McGROTTY
AND
LUDMILLA

Born in 1934, Alasdair Gray graduated in design and mural painting from the Glasgow School of Art. Since 1981, when *Lanark* was published by Canongate, he has authored, designed and illustrated seven novels, several books of short stories, a collection of his stage, radio and TV plays and a book of his visual art, *A Life in Pictures*. In November 2019, he received a Lifetime Achievement award from the Saltire Society. He died in December 2019, aged eighty-five.

ALSO BY ALASDAIR GRAY

McGROTTY
AND
LUDMILLA
or
THE HARBINGER REPORT

ALASDAIR
GRAY

CANONGATE

This Canons edition published in 2021 by Canongate Books Ltd,
14 High Street, Edinburgh EH1 1TE

First published in 1990 by Dog & Bone Press

Distributed in the USA by Publishers Group West
and in Canada by Publishers Group Canada

canongate.co.uk

1

British Library Cataloguing-in-Publication Data
A catalogue record for this book is available on request
from the British Library

ISBN 978 1 83885 387 7

Typeset in Times New Roman by 3btype.com

Printed and bound in Great Britain by Clays Ltd, Elcograf S.p.A

TO THE ONLY
BEGETTER • OF
THIS • ENSUING
ROMANCE
ANGEL
ALL
HAPPINESS
AND
THAT • ETERNITY
OUR • BIGHEADED
AUTHOR • WISHES
THE • WELLWISHING
PUBLISHER
SETTING
FORTH

TABLE OF

CONTENTS

1

THE MINISTRY OF SOCIAL STABILITY was created at the end of the nineteenth century to counteract the damage done by the spread of literacy and the granting of the vote to all male householders. Its marble-floored corridors, panelled in mahogany, still have the polished gleam they possessed when Victoria reigned. Those who work here are as wealthy as their predecessors of the last century, though they often deny it. They believe the loss of a world-wide colonial empire is an accident which befell less essential ministries. Their job is still to discipline, depress, pacify or (in years of crisis when the nation must move as one) bribe the poorer half of the British electorate.

Along one of these corridors two senior officials walked at an unhurried, thoughtful pace, for they were just digesting a good lunch taken at a nearby club. They discussed the long-awaited Harbinger Report, or rather, one discussed while the other made listening sounds.
"Every organization needs a great deal of corruption, of course, to stop it becoming rigid, callous and inefficient,"

said Arthur Shots, "But even corruption can be carried too far."

He was a pompous big man, but too competent, too rich, too dangerously selfish to be a figure of fun.

"I find that worrying," said Charlie Gold, who was less weighty than Shots, and knew it, and always told him as little as possible.

"Impeachment is still an ugly word," said Shots. "Everybody knows the Foreign Office is a pretty sinister show. You and I know it's an innocent babe in arms compared with the R.S.P.C.A."

"I find that very worrying."

"Poor Harbinger!" said Shots, with a sigh.

"Why poor?"

"He's near the brink."

"What brink?"

"He's on the verge."

"What verge?"

"Verge of crackup. Brink of breakdown."

"Well," said Gold, "I do find that very, very wo —"

Messages in this ministry are sent from office to office in steel cases secured by obsolescent brass padlocks. Sometimes new employees of the messenger grade try to show zeal by carrying them instead of pushing them in the trolleys provided. A figure, staggering from a side corridor with a stack of cases reaching to its nose, nearly trampled on Charlie Gold's foot.

"Mind where you're going!" cried Arthur Shots. The messenger recoiled violently in the wrong direction. His heel trampled hard on a different foot. Arthur Shots' public school training had made a stoic of him but the pain was unexpected and his deafening scream quite natural. He hopped on the uninjured foot, feeling the other for broken bones. The messenger, by a clumsy kind of jig, managed to stop the stack of cases toppling then retreated sideways down the corridor saying, "I didnae do that deliberately, you know! All the same, I'm sorry! I mean, I really am sorry!"

His grieved, indignant tone suggested his own foot had been trampled on. Shots' enraged glare turned to mere distaste, and then astonishment at finding himself so close to one so dishevelled and gaunt.

"I mean," bleated the messenger in a voice which grew louder and more bitter the further he receded, "if you want me to whine and grovel I'll whine and grovel but it'll do no good! None at all!"

He turned a corner. Shots looked to Gold for an explanation. "I'm afraid he's attached to my office," said Gold with sincere regret. "Been with me a week. He's a hopeless case. I doubt if he'll last."

"Hopeless is he? Hm," said Shots, and entered his own office.

2

THE OUTER ROOM WAS OCCUPIED by Miss Panther, Sir Arthur's principal secretary. She did not type or take dictation but received, phoned, dictated, and often sat perfectly still, waiting. She wore a black suit. Her smooth, unlined face could have been any age between thirty and sixty. Arthur Shots and she worked well together. He did not understand her and did not need to. She understood him thoroughly.

She was waiting when he limped past her desk to his inner office. They exchanged no sign until suddenly, as if struck by a thought, he turned and asked, "Anything doing, Miss Panther?"

Her voice was gentle, distinct, inflexible.

"I'm afraid not, Sir Arthur. Someone's secretary phoned but said there was nothing doing."

"I can wait."

He hitched a buttock and thigh over a corner of the desk, switched on a bright smile and looked down at her. She looked straight back with no change of expression. He said, "You and I have seen a great deal of foul weather together,

Miss Panther. Remember the Loch Ness oil leak? And the scandal over the rogue-virus shares which nearly put the whole nation in quarantine? Material has lain upon this desk"—he thumped it—"which could have provoked revolutions, overturned governments and made you a very rich woman. But you have never once given me cause to doubt your loyalty. You are discretion itself."

"Thank you, Sir Arthur."

"I mention this because I intend to question you on a matter so seemingly trivial that you might mention it casually to someone and I want that not to happen."

She said, "It shall not happen, Sir Arthur."

"Who is the Scotchman with the disgusting necktie?"

"He is called Mungo McGrotty."

"Clever, is he?"

"I gather not, Sir Arthur."

"Just average intelligence then?"

"I gather not, Sir Arthur."

"Surely he shows *some* symptoms of low animal cunning?"

"I gather not even that, Sir Arthur."

"Then how did he get here?"

She reminded him that the last Minister of Social Stability had been criticised in the House for employing nobody but Etonians, so the present Minister sometimes employed people with no kind of background in order not to seem elitist. He preferred them to be fools because clever ones daunted him. Shots paced up and down the room then said, very deliberately, "Miss Panther, I want to know more of this fellow. Fetch me his file and anything else you can discreetly discover."

He turned toward the inner office but she said, "Sir Arthur!" so he looked back. She stood behind the desk holding out a brown manila folder. She said, "I think this contains all you wish to know about Mungo McGrotty." He raised his eyebrows and took the folder saying with emphasis, *"Thank you,* Miss Panther."

He left the room and she sat down to wait again. Astonishing Arthur Shots was one of her satisfactions. Another was the cool aesthetic pleasure she found in helping him weave a fine web which only they perceived. It was invisible to the human flies trapped therein.

3

A WEEK LATER, MUNGO McGROTTY pushed a rubber-wheeled trolley into Miss Panther's room. A single padlocked dispatch box lay on the upper surface. He shifted it to her desk, grinning and shrugging like one underling to another. He said, "Something inside this is for Sir Shots. It's supposed to be sort of urgent. Well, anyway, that's what old Charlie thinks."

She told a telephone receiver, "He's here, Sir Arthur," then pointed to the door of the further room saying, "Go in there, please. No! Leave the dispatch box. It's you he wants."

"Eh? Oh."

The desk was not the main feature of Arthur Shots' inner office. In a braided smoking jacket, with a folder of papers open on his knees, he sat in the corner of a large leather-covered settee.

"Honest," said McGrotty. "It wasnae deliberate."

"I beg your pardon?"

"I did NOT deliberately stamp on your foot."

"But I'm glad you stamped on my foot. It forced me to notice you and I was struck by something in your face."

Sir Arthur turned to the intercom on his desk and told it,

"Isolate us, Miss Panther. Mungo and I must not be disturbed."

He replaced the receiver and pointed to the seat beside him saying, "Sit down. I've been looking through your file. It confirms what I suspected. Your father was the best friend I ever had."

"My father? But he — he —"

"Died before you were born. I know. Sit!"

"But he" said McGrotty, sitting and shaking his head, "he was a — was only a —"

"Sergeant in the Pay Corps. And I was a Colonel in the R.E.M.E. But three days after the Normandy landing he saved my life. You need a drink."

Shots shut the folder and went to a waist-high globe of the world saying, "Have you preferences?"

"I could do with a can of Export."

Shots slid back Canada and a wedge of the Arctic. Glasses and bottles gleamed in the cavity. He said, "I am pouring you a gin and tonic, this tête-à-tête must not be smelled afterwards on your breath. I suppose you know all about it? The war in France, I mean."

"No, I don't read books."

"I'm glad to hear it," said Shots, putting a glass in McGrotty's hand. "They can be terribly misleading. Take a cigar. There's a lighter. I am going to tell you the full story so listen carefully."

The settee faced a marble fireplace where flames flickered from gas burners among stones which McGrotty mistook for coal. Shots placed an elbow on the overmantle and spoke with the ease of one who enjoys telling elaborate stories.

"In the late autumn of '44, I was reconnoitring several miles in advance of our front line. My men didn't like it, the top brass didn't like it, and Jerry sure as hell didn't like it, but it kept me on my toes. Picture a gleaming wet blackness punctuated by the kapow! kapow! of the tracers and the sinister whine of the howitzers. In the middle stands a sinister geological formation with a crevasse in the side. The Mexicans call them *arroyos*. My instinct told me to give it a miss. My duty was to investigate. I was about to enter when I was prevented by a hand placed flat on the centre of my chest. It belonged to a weazened little runt of a fellow, one of those wretched, twisted splinters of humanity which our industrial slums spew forth in such abundance. North of the Tweed you call them *bauchles**"—McGrotty looked puzzled—"The Germans call them poison dwarfs, but of course they are the salt of the earth. In a gesture more eloquent than words the wee chap just — pointed. My foot! Had been about to descend! Into a heap of BLITZLICHTPULVERUM, the beastliest boobytrap in the whole hellish arsenal of the Hun. That *bauchle*, Mungo, was your father."

He stared solemnly at McGrotty, who stared back with open mouth.

"That was the last I saw of him," said Shots more casually. "A fortnight later I heard that, ironically enough, he had

---

* *According to the Shorter Aberdonian Scottish Dictionary a* bauchle *is an old shoe; a slipper down-at-heel; a person or thing of nought; a laughing stock; a clumsy person. This usage has for years been obsolete, except in very remote agricultural districts. Shots' acquaintance with it suggests he was nurtured by a nanny from Clackmannanshire.*

managed to get himself wiped out by the same Bosche
booby-trap at the Battle of the Bulge. Please don't drop ash
on the carpet."

McGrotty, much moved, laid down the cigar and untasted
glass and said tearfully, "I never realized my Dad was that
kind of bloke."

Shots gave him time to recover before sitting beside him
and asking on a sprightly note, "Like working here?"

"The money's alright."

"Made friends?"

"No, but it doesnae bother me. I'm used to not having
friends. At home nobody liked me because they thought
I was stuck up. Here nobody likes me because I'm not
stuck up enough."

"Good!" said Shots, and punched himself in the chest.
"I will befriend you. The debt I owe your father shall be
repaid, with interest, to you. I am going to have you
promoted, and rapidly; but, Mungo, I must toil for you
behind the scenes! No word of this special connection
between us must get about. I make that a test of your
loyalty. Your father's loyalty knew no bounds. Does yours?"

"Eh?" said McGrotty, confused by the complexities of this
question.

"I mean," said Shots patiently, "can you keep your mouth
shut about — us?"

"Oh yeah!"

"You should find it easy to be discreet. You have no friends.
Don't make any. You are used to being uninteresting. Stay
uninteresting and I can make you rich."

McGrotty was moved to tears again. He said, "You're being
very nice to me, Sir Shots, and I don't know what to say.
Can I call you Uncle Arthur, Sir Shots?"

"Just call me *Sir* Arthur, McGrotty," said Shots kindly.

"Thank you, Sir Arthur. And can I phone my Mammy and tell her the good news?"

"No! Not even your . . . Mammy McGrotty. Never trust a woman, McGrotty. Better trot off now. Charlie must not wonder where you've got to."

At the office door Shots gave McGrotty one of his bright sudden smiles and a warm firm shake of the hand. It filled McGrotty with a feeling of childlike peace and security.

4

THE MINISTER OF SOCIAL STABILITY called a meeting of his departmental chiefs to discuss Harbinger's fourth failure to deliver his report on an agreed deadline. The Minister badly wanted an excuse he could give to the Prime Minister.

"Tell her what Harbinger told you. Say he's a sick man," said Charlie Gold.

"I've told her that three times already," said the Minister, "and I don't even know what he's sick *of.* Nobody informs me of anything, least of all Harbinger."

"Ask Harbinger to send in a doctor's certificate," murmured someone else.

"But that will make me look like a common schoolteacher trying to trap a truant."

As usual the Minister's meeting ended inconclusively and as usual Gold and Shots returned from it together, for their offices were on the same corridor.

"I'm more worried than ever about Harbinger. What has he unearthed?" said Gold. Shots' attitude had mellowed since they last discussed the topic.

"If he's dug deep enough to implicate himself nobody

need worry," he said. "But I have something to confess to you, Charlie. I believe in fair play."

"You do?"

"Two weeks ago, in this very corridor, on this very spot!" They came to a halt. "I collided with a young Scot who made a very poor impression on me."

"McGrotty. He's in his thirties," murmured Gold.

"He's young at heart," Sir Arthur assured him. "Young where it counts. And so refreshingly naive! Never judge by first impressions, Charlie! I've since had a word with the lad — in private — and he interests me, strangely."

"Oh."

"Yes, he's a rough diamond, but don't you feel he's wasted as a messenger?"

"It . . . hadn't occurred to me."

"Frankly," murmured Shots, "I would like to encounter him in a sphere closer to our own. Know what I mean?"

"Yes."

"Anyway!" said Shots, stretching his arms like one who has cast off a load. "His future is in your hands, Charlie. He has depths, that youth. Someone ought to plumb them."

But the load Arthur Shots had cast on Charlie Gold was heavier than Gold could carry by himself. That evening he rushed to share it with his friend Aubrey Rose, who sat at a table for two in a corner of their club dining room.

"Listen to this!" said Gold without preamble, sitting opposite him. "Bloody Arthur Shots was onto me today and — I can hardly believe it. You know that horrible Grotty thing they've given me? Arthur is interested in him! Strangely! Wants me to promote him!"

"Impossible," said Rose. "Grotty's not even pretty."

"I know."

"Besides," said Rose, "small girls, not rough trade, are Arthur's foible. Wasn't there once something between him and the Minister's daughter?"

"He's past his prime, of course, like all of us," said Gold, sighing. "He called McGrotty a rough diamond, with depths, and told me to bring him into our sphere."

"I'm not taking him."

"Who will?"

"Give him to Granny."

"Give him to the Minister? How can I?"

"Tell Granny what Arthur told you, rough diamond with depths et cetera. Tell him we can't afford to be elitist nowadays. We can, of course, but the Minister has learned nothing since the sixties."

"So I can still bully him with bolshie rot like that?"

"Oh yes."

"Well, that's a weight off my mind." said Gold, and studied the menu.

5

THE MINISTER'S OFFICE HAD TWO outer rooms. His principal secretary, Mrs Bee, occupied one and a permanent typist the other. The typist's room held the office safe and a desk for an auxiliary typist if pressure of work required that. There had been no such emergencies for many years, so Mungo McGrotty was installed at the extra desk as the Minister's messenger. The Minister pointed out to Charlie Gold (who suggested this arrangement) that he did not need and did not want a messenger.

"People like you need messengers," said the Minister, "because you keep sending messages to me and to each other. I send messages to nobody but the Prime Minister, when she wants one, and they go by external courier. Why create a sinecure?"

"We feel the dignity of your office requires it."

"Don't be silly."

"McGrotty may be a rough diamond but it doesn't do to be elitist."

"You have not answered my question!" said the Minister, with one of the rare flashes of acumen which made him unpredictable.

"The fact is," said Charlie Gold, who had no aptitude for lying, "I want McGrotty promoted out of my office into yours. This is not, not, not, (I promise you) not because McGrotty is an unmitigated social disaster, though he is, of course. McGrotty has become the, er, special boyfriend of Arthur Shots. Shots has asked me to get him promoted. I'm shit scared of upsetting Arthur Shots."

"So am I," admitted the Minister. He frowned for a while then smiled and at last chortled, saying, "So old Arthur is a — ! So perhaps Arthur has always been a — ! Dear dear dear. My my my. Well, if promoting McGrotty will keep Arthur sweet, let's do it."

"Thanks awfully, Bill," said Gold with heartfelt enthusiam, "You *are* a likeable chap."

The Minister blushed and looked away.
He liked to be likeable, though he knew this was
a weakness.

6

AT FIRST MUNGO LOATHED PROMOTION. Only a sophisticated education or a lack of energy equip folk for salaried unemployment. McGrotty, the illegitimate only child of a self-sacrificing and aspiring office cleaner, had been taught to work and was not without energy. He lacked imagination and understanding because his schools had discouraged these, but he had easily come first in examinations because these had been mainly memory exercises and McGrotty could remember in detail anything he heard or read, if it was untainted by fancy. A prosperous parent could have made him a chartered surveyor or accountant. He entered the lowest grade of the civil service and became a filing clerk in a Social Stability office: first in the Motherwell district, then at the Strathclyde Regional Headquarters in Glasgow.

He enjoyed the work. Before his office uneasily converted itself to the use of word processors he filed and retrieved information with the ease and speed of the most modern models. This embarrassed his superiors, for nobody wanted part of their office so efficient that it was out of line with the rest. They could have kept McGrotty in line by promoting him beyond his limit of efficiency, but that would have made him one of themselves and he was not likeable. He knew it, but did not know how to change, and deliberately exaggerated his unlikeable qualities to show he did not care. This act fooled nobody and made him ugly company, so he kept being transferred to better paid jobs in more important offices, but at the same low grade of service. From the Strathclyde Regional Headquarters he went to Saint Andrew's House in Edinburgh and thence to the Ministry at Whitehall, though the Scottish Under-Secretary of State exerted pressure for six years before getting London to take him.

And now McGrotty sat feeling lonely and useless at the unneeded desk in the Minister's outermost office. The young typist who shared the room clearly thought him an intruder and found, or pretended to find, his accent unintelligible. When the trolley lady brought mid-morning or mid-afternoon tea the typist carried her cup and biscuit into Mrs Bee's room without a word. On the third day McGrotty entered Mrs Bee's room himself and said desperately, "Listen, can I file something for you? I'm good at that."
She stared at him.
He said, "I'll do anything, anything you want! Short of murder. Please give me something to do."

Mrs Bee pondered. The principal secretaries did all the ministers' practical work at a level which the Minister and departmental heads hardly noticed. The one exception was Arthur Shots who, in a quiet way they greatly appreciated, kept in touch with all the principal secretaries.

"Well," said Mrs Bee, "I cannot give you steel boxes to wheel about, but you can run errands for me if that is not beneath your dignity."

"Listen, don't be sarcastic!" said McGrotty. "You know I've no dignity, I know I've no dignity, so don't be sarcastic."

Mrs Bee looked at him closely. Though the mother of three grown-up sons, she was still a motherly woman and supported an organization which cared for stray dogs. McGrotty reminded her of an ill-treated Afghan hound. She suddenly wanted to be kind to him and said, "Our office has many dealings with the office of your friend Sir Arthur Shots. We can contrive things so that you are able to see him quite often — as often as you wish."

"Sir Shots is not —" said McGrotty, then stopped, because she seemed to know something. He said cautiously, "Sir Shots is not supposed to be my friend."

"You have nothing to be ashamed of!" Mrs Bee assured him. "Sir Arthur is privileged. He is a cousin of the Queen. Of course he must avoid publicity, so your secret is safe with us. Take this note to Petal Pargetter of the

Greenpeace-Sewage Interface, room eight-oh-three."

7

AND ON THE FIFTH DAY LUDMILLA entered the room, stopped halfway across it and stared. McGrotty stared back. For a while neither quite believed the reality of who they saw. Ludmilla looked like a ravishingly lovely child who had been badly knocked about and deprived of decent clothes by a cruel stepmother in a Cinderella pantomine. After a while he saw that her bruised, swollen-looking eyelids and mouth were tinted with lavender makeup and purple lipstick, that her blonde hair had not been wrenched to one side by a strong hand and ruthlessly knotted above her ear but carefully combed and set to appear so, that her small tight skirt and jacket were not dirty canvas but unevenly dyed suede exquisitely tailored to look as if she had outgrown them; that she was not barefoot but wore wedge-soled sandals held by thin transparent loops round each toe and heel. Her appearance of damsel in distress immediately dazzled him. On noticing the time, wealth and art she had used to create it, he was dazzled still more. He wished to grovel before her but did not know how to start.

"You're new here!" she said at last, making that sound like an accusation. He could only nod. "Why do you wear that terrible tie?"

"It wasnae deliberate — I'm bad at choosing things."

"Then get someone with an education to choose for you. And while they're doing it get them to buy you a suit that fits. Off-the-peg stuff lets down the tone of the office dreadfully. People notice these things. I know Daddy is the reverse of a glamorous Minister but you're paid to support him and paid adequately, I think."

She stepped briskly into Mrs Bee's room leaving the door open. He heard her say, "Hello, Bee! I've got to see Daddy."

"Oh please don't go into his room just now! The Prime Minister is on the line to him."

"But I must see him. Mummy sent me."

He heard the innermost door banged open and slammed shut.

8

MRS BEE SENT A NOTE TO MISS Panther and Miss Panther said to McGrotty, who delivered it, "Sir Arthur is expecting you." McGrotty entered Shots' room with no special feelings. His connection with Shots had added no joy to his life. When Shots asked pleasantly, "How are you doing, my boy?" he answered without enthusiasm, "Apart from folk making remarks about my clothes it's alright I suppose. The extra money is good. I suppose I've got you to thank."

"Don't mention it," said Shots, handing him a gin and tonic and sinking into a corner of the settee. "Your career is only begining. In a year or two, or a month or two, or in as little as a few days, a chance may arrive for me to do you some *real* good. Your salary could be doubled. Or would you prefer a lump sum? Fifty thousand tax free, say? Think about it."

"In a few days?" said McGrotty, overwhelmed.

"It is possible."

"But how . . . ?"

"Shhh!" whispered Shots. "When the time comes I will ask you to do a very simple, easy little thing, something that won't take more than a minute. And when you have done it Miss Panther will hand you a packet wrapped in sky blue paper containing fifty thousand pounds in notes and we'll have another discussion about your future. Meanwhile here is the card of the only tailor in London worth cultivating. Phone him today. Make an appointment. Say I recommended you and leave the rest to him."

"Can I sit down?" said McGrotty, and sat down. "You see there is this girl, oh, a gorgeous girl, a girl I would like to —"

"There may," murmured Shots, bringing his lips close to McGrotty's ear, "be a tiny element of risk."

"Risk?"

"A tiny element. But you have placed your future in my hand, so if you obey me nothing really bad can happen. If you disobeyed me I would let you go and then you would smash. You wouldn't like that. It would be letting your father down, and he had such *hopes* for you."

"But he died —"

"Before you were born," said Shots impatiently. "Of course of course. But he suspected that something like you was on the way."

"I feel you have taken his place, Sir Arthur," said McGrotty moistly. Shots almost gagged with revulsion at the thought but disguised this with a grin. He said, "Quite right, quite right, but there's no need to blub about it. Off you go."

But before McGrotty reached the door Sir Arthur called him back and asked if he had ever read Orwell's delightful novel, *1984*.

"I sat my A-levels on it."

"You remember that amusing interview between O'Brien and Winston when O'Brien holds up two fingers?"

"Yes."

"How many fingers am I holding up, McGrotty?" asked Shots.

McGrotty peered closely, then said, "Two, Sir Arthur?"

"Correct. But what if I told you the actual number was three? What would you say then?"

McGrotty thoughtfully scratched the stubble on his cheek and at last said, "I would say there was something wrong with my seeing, Sir Arthur."

Shots laughed aloud, slapped his thigh and said, "Good lad! You'll do. Trot along."

But when McGrotty had left, Arthur Shots grew serious, almost morose. He had forged a strong chain to bind a nation. McGrotty was the only link he had not tested, and could not test, before he started to tighten that chain.

9

THERE WAS SOMETHING ROTTEN in the State of Britain. Rumours of it had not reached the general public, who had come to accept a degree of social rottenness which would have frightened it ten or twenty years earlier. Even so, a part of the public that worked in government offices sensed something new and sinister in high places and did not want it to spread. Several principal secretaries suggested that, without risking a public enquiry, the Civil Service could put its house in order. Discreet, dependable people from the middle echelons of each ministry should be promised anonymity if they wrote memos describing what they knew. These memos should be sent to one of themselves: a discreet dependable man whose honesty nobody would question: somebody like Geoffrey Harbinger of Architectural Ecology. Harbinger had no political allegiances, no shares in big companies, no odd sexual habits and no friends in high places. He lived with his widowed sister. His private life was a sequence of harmless hobbies. He could report secretly on the letters and pass the report to the cabinet by way of Downing Street.

The Social Stability Minister accumulated details of this scheme without noticing where he had picked them up. He was an innocent soul and thought it a good scheme. Architectural Ecology was an autonomous department but came under Social Stability, so he raised the matter at a cabinet meeting. The discussion which followed showed that his colleagues had already discussed the scheme privately. Some even approved of it, though each wanted the report made by one of their own departmental heads. The project nearly foundered on this division, especially after the fourth meeting when the P.M. called it a waste of time. At this point the Social Stability Minister, sweating with embarassment, explained that perhaps he should mention — he hoped there was nothing in it — maybe it was mere alarmist gossip — but a source of information he had hitherto found wholly reliable —

"What source of information?" asked the P.M.

"My secretary," said the Minister blushing. "She is friendly with the secretary of a, er, a senior civil servant of almost ministerial rank, someone too well connected to be afraid of the Official Secrets Act, someone who is one of us, in a way —"

"Come to the point," said the P.M. "Exactly what did Arthur Shots' secretary tell your secretary?"

"She said Arthur had worrying information he wanted to pass on to someone, and if he couldn't give it to Harbinger he might leak it."

"Leak it to who? What does this sinister information relate to? Why won't he bring it to me?"

"My secretary didn't say," said the Minister miserably. "And officially, you see, I am quite in the dark. And unofficially I know nothing certain."

"Alright," said the P.M. after a long pause. "Tell Harbinger the glad tidings. No, don't. I'll tell him the glad tidings. Tomorrow. Then tell the informers in your ministries to get in touch with him."

10

SOME MONTHS BEFORE THIS CABINET meeting Geoffrey Harbinger was puzzled to find himself the subject of articles in the press. The *Observer* colour supplement described a day in his life under a photograph of him beside a bookshelf holding an early *Decameron* bound in calfskin by Claude de Picques.

"Why write about me?" he asked the journalist who interviewed him. "I am not an important figure."

"Someone suggested you to the editor," said the journalist, "and it's a good idea. The colour comics are full of professional exhibitionists. A modest bachelor who collects books and sings in a church choir may not be important but makes a very nice change."

A few weeks later an article in *New Society* began by saying, "To do an essential job quietly and well is no way to attract attention nowadays, and few people know even the name of Geoffrey Harbinger." It went on to suggest that Harbinger was the main force behind the gracious new liberalism which was breathing life into British building design. Harbinger knew this was untrue. His department had been created by a Labour administration when a lot of housing was being built with public funds. Architectural Ecology had powers in those days, but had been stripped of them by the time Harbinger took charge. His team of experts still looked at the plans of new buildings and suggested changes to make them harmonise with surroundings and serve the convenience of those who lived nearby, but the suggestions could not be enforced so were usually ignored. The most effective thing he did was give an inscribed silver dish to the architects of buildings which seemed less horrid than usual. He thought the new liberalism in British architecture was a crazy fashion for grotesquely irrelevant surface complications, and not his fault at all.

Then the gossip pages of a popular newspaper started printing photographs of him walking with his dog, bidding for a rare volume at an auction or going to Easter service at Saint Frideswide with his ten-year-old niece. All these photos had captions which took his importance for granted while referring to his modesty, dependability and honesty. This worried him. He was not more honest than others, though he would have liked to be. He disliked the perquisites of his office, especially an iniquitous but perfectly legal tax-avoidance dodge which gave him an unearned extra income in return for a small deduction from his monthly salary. If he opted out of it he would seem to be criticising his colleagues, some of whom also felt uneasy about the dodge. He tried to assuage his guilt with donations to charity and by investing in corporations which did not directly profit from armaments, apartheid and pollution; but he doubted if God was tricked by such tactics. And then the Prime Minister summoned him to Downing Street.

Her first words were, "I hope you know what you're in for."
He did not. She explained, and he was overwhelmed:
overwhelmed by the honour of the trust bestowed on him
and by the staggering intelligence of she who bestowed it.
She had never met him before this moment, yet across the
acres of offices dividing them she had seen that he and he
alone was the conscientious doctor who could isolate the
infection which threatened the nation's life: an infection he
had never suspected — hitherto he had only encountered
iniquity in its legal and venerated forms. He was too
overwhelmed to notice the hostility in her manner, though
the day before his death, recalling the interview in detail, he
saw she had spoken as if he had *manoeuvred* her into giving
him the job. He left Downing Street that morning in a daze
of wonder and delight. The Harbinger Report would not be
public knowledge at first because only the mighty would read
it, but it would eventually earn him a shining page in the social
history of Britain. He suddenly felt sorry he was childless. His
children would have grown up to be proud of him.

11

AND NOW HE TALKED ALOUD TO himself without knowing it, and could not sleep without taking pills, and had flung the pills away because insomnia was preferable to nightmares. He kept dreaming he sat at his desk, staring at an envelope containing the Report. Gradually he dreamed something dreadful had arrived. Reluctantly raising his head, he saw a mass had swelled up beneath the office carpet, a mass with a distinct shape to which the carpet adhered. At first it looked like an octopus with tentacles as thick as human bodies, but with a little jerk it slid an inch toward him and he saw it was a huge, amputated, living human hand. It continued crawling toward him in little jerks, swelling larger as it did so. The door was on the far side of it. Behind him was an open window onto an endless drop through an infinite void.

He really was sitting at his desk staring at an envelope containing the Report, but he had not slept for forty-eight hours. He feared to raise his head in case he saw the hand with his waking eyes. The phone rang. His secretary told him the Minister was on the line. The Minister said, "Harbinger. Your Report. When."

"Well, you see, Minister —"

"The P.M.'s been onto me about it, the F.O.'s been onto me about it, all sorts of bodies are nag-nag-nagging me and you do nothing but procrastinate."

"I'm not well, Minister."

"Well, I'm sorry you aren't well," said the Minister without sympathy. "Why aren't you well?"

"I'm distressed by my Report. It incriminates many decent, public-spirited necessary people. Famous people. Some of the highest and best-loved names in Britain."

"I don't care how distressing your Report is! We, not you, are paid to suppress the facts. When can we have them? When? When? When?"

Harbinger sighed and whispered, "Today."

"Really?"

"The manuscript is on my desk."

"Manuscript?"

"I could not let a typist see it, but you will find my handwriting painfully legible. There is no copy. I have burned all notes for this Report, and all letters from my informants. Whatever the public consequences, *they* must not suffer."

"You thoughtful fellow!" said the Minister cheerfully. "Send it off at once to the P.M."

"I am sending it to you."

"Why?"

"Read and discover."

"How intriguing! I won't be in the office today, I'm going down to Wales to open the Rhonda Valley Nature Reserve, but I'll peep into it first thing tomorrow. Goodbye, Harbinger."

"Minister!" said Harbinger in a broken voice. "If anything happens, tell them I tried."

"I don't follow you, Harbinger. If anything happens to what, tell them you tried what? I suggest you send me the Report, take an aspirin and go to bed."

Harbinger sat for a long time then said, "The evil that men do lives after them, rough hew them how we may. Their virtues we write in water, with a bare bodkin."

He stood up, locked the envelope in a dispatch box and got his secretary to summon an external courier. The courier arrived, chained the box to his wrist and departed. Harbinger kept the key. For security reasons he would send it by a different courier as soon as Mrs Bee received the box. There could be no rest before he knew his Report had been transferred to the Minister's safe so he paced about the room, moaning and trying to remember things which had once made him happy. "I believe in God the Father Almighty, Maker of Heaven and Earth," he said, "and in Jesus Christ His only Son our Lord, the rough male kiss of blankets, good strong thick stupefying incense smoke and jellies soother than the creamy curd. But my head knows too much."

He closed his eyes, beat his brows with his fists, cried, "*PANTOCRATORAPHORBIA!*" in a kind of howling whisper, then shed passionate tears.

"I believe," he said, recovering a little, "in the Fellowship of the Holy Ghost, the Holy Catholic Church, the Communion of Saints, the proud man's contumely, the insolence of office and the spurns which patient merit of the unworthy take. But trailing clouds of glory do we come from God who is our home beside the lake, beneath the trees, fluttering and dancing in the bee-loud glade. And I shall have some peace there."

Mrs Bee phoned to say she had the box. Harbinger called his secretary, gave her the key and said, "You know where to send this, Miss Soames. Tell me when it gets there, Miss Soames, and then . . . put out the light and then put out *thy* light."

"I don't understand you, Mr Harbinger."

"Tell me when it gets there. We have done the state some service in our time, Miss Soames."

"Are you quite well, Mr Harbinger?"

"Yes."

He sat at his desk in a sick stupor, willing his eyes and ears to stay open until the call came which told him the key was with Mrs Bee. The call came. He sighed, stood up, took off his jacket, folded it neatly and laid it on the carpet. He opened a drawer in the desk and lifted out a pistol issued to him by the army in 1939. As a Home Guard lieutenant, then a captain in the Territorials, he was surely entitled to it. He knelt on the floor, clasped the pistol between his uplifted hands and whispered, "Sweet Jesus, save me."

He lay flat on his back with head on jacket, fitted the mouth of the barrel into his right ear and fired a bullet through his brain.

Miss Soames ran in. Like several other people she had expected him to die by an overdose of tranquillisers. She grabbed the phone, dialled and said, "Hilda."

"Mary. The Report?" asked Miss Panther.

"That's in the Minister's safe now, but Harbinger has shot himself! This minute! There's blood. Oh, I'm going to faint."

"Well done, Mary. Arthur won't forget you. Scream very loudly now. It will bring you to your senses and strike others as a womanly thing to do."

12

S O MISS PANTHER TOLD SIR ARTHUR,
"The Report is now locked in the Minister's safe."
"Good."
"And Geoffrey Harbinger has shot himself."
"Good. Good."
"And I am about to send for Mungo McGrotty."
"Excellent."

13

WELCOME AND CONGRATULATIONS, Mungo!" said Arthur Shots genially. "A certain sky blue packet awaits you in Miss Panther's desk. You will be a rich man when you leave the Ministry tonight."

"But what?" said Mungo. "What am I supposed to to to —"

"Do. Look at this envelope marked *Extra Top Secret and Confidential.* Is it familiar to you?"

"Half an hour ago Mrs Bee put one just like it in our office safe."

"Put this one in the large poacher's pocket in the lining of your brand new Savile Row suit."

The envelope seemed to contain a thick sheaf of paper. McGrotty had not thoroughly explored his new suit. He was astonished to find an interior pocket which the envelope perfectly fitted.

"Now listen carefully, Mungo!" said Shots. "You will leave here and return to your office at exactly one minute past five. The Minister's secretary will be impatiently awaiting you, for the other staff will have left. You will tell her I have asked you to read and memorise the secret oxygen famine plans for an emergency meeting tonight at the Air Ministry —"

"But that's not true!"

"She will open the safe," said Shots loudly, "hand you the plans and hover nearby while you read them! Suddenly the telephone rings in her office next door. It is her job to answer that phone. It is also her job to be present when the safe is open. She decides to trust you, and goes out to the phone, but, Mungo! You are not the harmless idiot she supposes! You step to the safe and switch the envelope inside with the one in your pocket. The operation takes four seconds. A minute later the secretary returns. You hand back the oxygen famine plans and return here, to me, at once. Six months later your name appears in the New Year Honours list."

"But that's *stealing!*" said McGrotty.

Shots chuckled in a friendly way. He said, "I am surprised, Mungo, to hear you employ such an unscientific word. You will not be '*stealing*' the document in question. You will simply be transferring it from one office to another as cautiously as possible."

"But why?" said McGrotty.

"Mungo!" said Shots gravely. "The United Kingdom will be in terrible danger if that document falls into the wrong hands. Without doubt certain self-seeking, unscrupulous men dearly wish to get hold of it and the Minister's safe is not burglar-proof. The fact that you will bring the envelope here tonight demonstrates that. For years I have prayed for this chance of exposing the inadequacy of our security arrangements. Will you help me, Mungo?"

McGrotty shook his head and said, "There's something about this I don't get, Arthur."

"Then I overrated your intelligence!" cried Shots fiercely, "I thought you were clever enough to know there were things you could never *get*, Mungo, things you must leave to me. Well, I was wrong. You are an unpatriotic donkey with the guts of a louse and not the faintest notion of which side your bread is buttered!"

He sat down on the sofa, folded his arms and said quietly, "Please go away, Mungo."

McGrotty could not quite do so.

"I don't like disappointing you, Arthur," he admitted.

"That shows there are sparks of decency in you. Unluckily they are feeble sparks. I'm not angry, Mungo, but I had looked forward to rewarding your loyalty. Fifty thousand pounds is very little money nowadays, but it would have been a start. Leave me, Mungo, I . . . can't pretend I'm not . . . wounded."

McGrotty sighed, gulped, then said, "I'll do it."

"Yes!" said Shots, springing up and bestowing one of his firm, fortifying handclasps. "Yes, you *will* do it. Don't try to *think*, McGrotty. I have thought for you. Just act and I will be able to make you a rich, famous, popular and completely contented man. But first — while we wait for five o' clock — I will give you a taste of your native Drambuie and tell you another tale of your father's loyalty."

Arthur Shots' rhetoric had perhaps been enfeebled by overuse. McGrotty was too worried to attend closely to the other tale of his father's loyalty, and did not find what he heard of it convincing.

14

"HERE THEY ARE," SAID MRS BEE, handing him a folder, "the secret neutron-flux umbrella plans."

"I — er — actually asked," said McGrotty, "for the secret oxygen famine plans."

"Granny keeps them in the same folder," said Mrs Bee. "We are short of folders. I must order more."

McGrotty pulled out some typed sheets and pretended to scan them with one eye while examining the depths of the safe with the other. Like all the Ministry's machines which did not serve the comfort of senior officials the safe was old-fashioned and far too big. He saw five deep shelves, four of them empty. Folders with code numbers on their spines were stacked on the middle shelf beside a franking machine, an iron tray piled with rubber stamps and a wire tray holding the envelope. A phone rang.

"Who can that be at five-past-five? I'll be back in a jiffy, Mr McGrotty," said Mrs Bee, and left the room.

McGrotty hesitated then plunged toward the safe.

"*Transferring not stealing,*" he thought frantically, putting the folder on a lower shelf to free his hands. "*Transferring not stealing —*"

"Hello, funny one!" said Ludmilla, entering. "What are you doing? Stealing state secrets?"
The adrenaline released by the shock of her arrival gave him some moments of self-possession. He fumbled a little then turned to her, straightening his jacket. He said sullenly, "Of course! That's what they pay me for. Why are you here anyway? Your Dad's in Wales."
She decided to treat his surliness as a challenge and leaned back against a desk, smiling at him and opening her ankle-length Arctic fox-fur coat. Today her lips were a thin scarlet, her sleek narrow dress the same colour. Between the two edges of the coat her body looked like a vivid snake with breasts. She said, "I left a purse in Daddy's office with lots and lots of money in it."
"Why did you call me funny one?"
"Because you're funny. You don't shave properly."
"I shave three times a day! It isnae my fault the stuff keeps sprouting."
"Grow a beard."
"And look like a poofy artist? No thanks!"
She giggled, opened her handbag and felt inside saying, "You also wear funny clothes."
"This suit cost four hundred guineas and was cut by the only tailor in London worth cultivating!"
"Yes," she said, lighting a cigarette, "I can see it's a good suit but on you it looks funny. It's your basic shape that's wrong."
His face went white at the cruelty of this. He said, "*You're* no oil painting if it comes to that!"

"If you mean I'm not attractive," she said, sweetly blowing a smoke ring, "why can't you take your eyes off me?"

He gasped as if punched in the stomach.

Mrs Bee bustled in. She said irritably, "Someone kept telling me to hold the line, then said they had the wrong number. Please hurry, Mr McGrotty, this is my bridge night."

"I am not made of wood!" yelled McGrotty. "I can't take any more! I can't, can't, WON'T!"

Half blind with tears of pain and rage, he blundered from the room and ran away.

The ladies looked at each other.

"He is funny!" said Ludmilla, laughing.

"I only told him to hurry," said Mrs Bee. She unlocked the Minister's room. Ludmilla collected her purse and left. A large man in the corridor outside looked as if he was lurking.

"Uncle Arthur!" cried Ludmilla.

He switched on the wide fake grin she had known since childhood. "Er, hello, Ludmilla. I'm waiting for the young McGrotty. To give him a lift to the Air Ministry, you know. Will he be long, do you think?"

"I made him hysterical and he ran away," said Ludmilla. "Take me out to dinner, Uncle Arthur."

"Ran away?" cried Shots hysterically. "Ran away with God urgent business Ludmilla what if he no it's too horrible oh poor bloody Britain!"

And he too ran away.

15

ARTHUR SHOTS CHARGED OUT INTO Whitehall, turned left, sprinted fifty yards along the pavement, stopped, turned, sprinted a hundred yards the opposite way, stopped, held his brow for five seconds then began hailing taxis.

While doing these things he was thinking that McGrotty had had no time to read the Report — that if McGrotty was caught quickly nothing catastrophic could happen. McGrotty lodged in a civil service hostel on Horseferry Road: if he wanted to read the Report he would surely do so there, but what if he went by bus and read it on the bus? MI5 said McGrotty did not visit pubs, but what if he read it in a Wimpy Bar? Surely not, but why not? What could a fool like McGrotty be trusted *not* to do when he stopped doing what he was told? For a moment Shots thought he glimpsed McGrotty strolling ahead of him (it was a bright evening in mid Autumn) reading the Report as he strolled and discarding pages into waste-paper bins. But McGrotty was hysterical, Ludmilla had said, speaking as though this was a joke. She must have intruded during the burglary, suspected nothing but scared McGrotty out of his wits. So McGrotty had not planned to cheat him: indeed he, Arthur Shots, had given McGrotty no time to plan anything. Only forty minutes had passed (they seemed like forty days) since he told McGrotty what to do: twelve minutes since he sent him to do it. So why had McGrotty not run to him? Could Ludmilla have scared him away before he pocketed the Report? Was the Report still in the safe? That would delay the completion of Shots' grand design but not destroy the global economy nor damage Shots socially. He would learn tomorrow if this were so: meanwhile he must act as if McGrotty had the Report on him and catch McGrotty before he found time to read it, even if he didn't have it. Because he might have it. How to catch him? MI5 had confirmed that McGrotty was friendless. The wisest thing was to go to McGrotty's hostel and, if he was not there, wait. Shots took a taxi, spoke to the hostel warden and found McGrotty had not returned. Shots was good with underlings. He told them nothing, never tipped, but led them to feel that helping him was a patriotic duty. The warden unlocked McGrotty's room with the hostel key and let Shots wait inside.

The next five hours were the dreariest of Shots' life. For the first hour it was possible to believe that McGrotty might arrive any moment. For the second and third hour it was impossible not to imagine him sitting somewhere, in a restaurant or a public library perhaps, reading the Report. After that Shots could not think what to imagine. He knew only part of what the Report contained and that part was enough to put an intelligent man in fear of his life. How would it strike McGrotty? Frantically, again and again, Shots examined the sparse contents of the room for a clue to the working of the fellow's mind. A large motor bicycle of Japanese make stood on blocks in a corner. It looked new from the shop, but small signs showed it had been well used and lovingly maintained. Beneath the bed were stacks of coloured cartoon magazines issued serially by an American publishing house. Judging by the numbers, McGrotty had been collecting them for over twenty years. Half depicted the adventures of Conan, a muscular thug who lived in a world of banal historical fantasies with a supernatural twist. The other half showed the adventures of Red Sonia, a well-built woman who wore just enough chain-mail to clothe her groin and breasts, had long red hair, a sword, and lived in the same sort of world as Conan the Barbarian. McGrotty was not wholly illiterate, for on the saddle lay a dog-eared paperback called *Zen and the Art of Motorcycle Maintenance*. The room had no pictures or ornaments. The only personal items were drab clothes in the wardrobe and an unfinished letter on the chest of drawers, dated the previous evening. The handwriting was large and backward-sloping, yet meticulously formed.

Dear Mum, (it said)

Well, here I am, transferred yet again. The Friend in High Places I told you about, and whose name I must not utter for political reasons, has been true to his word. So now I lord it in a Cabinet Minister's outer office though he is not a very glamourous minister, you will never see him on the telly. But financially I am better off than ever, we need have no fear of the future. You can stop the cleaning job whenever you like, though I respect your wish to Keep Working Right On to the End of the Road. Man does not live by money alone, where would we be without our daily darg?*

---

* Darg: *Day labour of a manually strenuous sort. (Scottish.)*

Socially speaking nothing has changed much. As far as I can see the manners of the English so-called upper classes get nastier the upper they are, especially the women. I wish there were hills here. In Motherwell or Glasgow or Edinburgh I could mount my trusty Hakagawa and take off for the tops of Tinto or the Campsies or Arthur's Seat and gaze down on the human anthills where I am usually a toiling unit on a nine-to-five basis. I could also gaze out and up across that universe which is mankind's greater home. These glimpses of eternity kept me sane. But there are no hills in London. What keeps me sane? My wee Mummy's love, and my expectation of further promotion in the near future.

Things are as bleak as ever on the romantic front. I know you will not die happy before you see me married to a real nice lassie, nice meaning posh with decent manners. But as I said before, (here a word starting with capital L had been scribbled over) *the women here get nastier the posher they are.*

Oh I wish I was the sort who

Shots read this letter several times. He dismissed McGrotty's glimpses of eternity as Wordsworthian claptrap picked up from an enthusiastic schoolteacher, but otherwise the letter was evidence of a naive but struggling intelligence. It was naive because it did not care how it appeared to others, so could not rise to that self-conscious positive, political awareness called cunning. This was comforting, but what if McGrotty had so far failed to be cunning because he had nothing to be cunning about? What if active intelligence depended on opportunity as much as heredity? Ulysses Grant was an alcoholic small-town shopkeeper before the American Civil War brought him forward as one of his nation's most brilliant military strategists.

At this point Shots found himself on the verge of panic. He stabilised himself by remembering that, even if McGrotty acted cunningly he could do nothing with the Report. He would not take it to the police because he had stolen it. He could not leak it to the press because it was covered by the Official Secrets Act. He could not sell it to a foreign power because he lacked contacts and any sort of support. For the same reason he could not blackmail those mentioned in it. The cunningest thing McGrotty could do was give the report to him, Arthur Shots, and apologise for the delay in passing it over. One thing Shots decided: when McGrotty returned and confronted him he, Shots, would give no sign of anger or anxiety, would make no demands and ask no questions. His mere presence in that room was a question in itself. He would leave McGrotty to do the talking.

16

AT QUARTER TO MIDNIGHT McGROTTY entered holding a pale yellow polystyrene disc and prising from its surface with his free hand a fragment of pizza, which fragment he bit and munched. He was surprised to see Arthur Shots, but not greatly surprised. He finished munching, said, "Oh, hullo, Arthur," and dropped the disc in a small bin.

Shots stood up and said hoarsely, *"Where is it, McGrotty?"*

He was wretchedly aware of not acting as he had planned.

"Take a seat, Arthur," said McGrotty, going to the wardrobe and removing his jacket. "Let's have a canna lager."

"Where is it, McGrotty?"

"It is not," said McGrotty, removing his jacket, "in the large poacher's pocket in the lining of my brand new, made-to-measure Savile Row suit." He displayed the lining, hung the jacket in the wardrobe, took two tins of beer from a shelf and offered one to Shots saying, "Sorry I cannae offer spirits — spirits go to my head."

"GIVE ME THE REPORT, McGROTTY!" yelled Shots. "NOW! AT ONCE! DO YOU HEAR ME?"

McGrotty sighed, shook his head slowly from side to side and again offered the tin of beer. Shots was appalled to see his own fingers close round and grip it.

"I'll tell you what I hate about London, Arthur," said McGrotty, looking straight into Arthur Shots' face. "Everyone tries to bully me here. Actually it was just the same in Scotland. My Mammy bullied me, my teachers, my bosses . . . I like you, Arthur, because you've treated me like an equal."

Shots shuddered. He saw in McGrotty's eyes a new-born gleam of self-conscious intelligence.

"Mungo," said Shots quietly. "The Report. Please. Where is it?"

"That's better!" said McGrotty. He lay on his bed, crossed his legs, opened the beercan, sipped from it and chuckled. "Ludmilla!" he said. "She's a warmer,* isn't she? I love that lassie. When I ran out of the Ministry tonight I wasn't avoiding you, Arthur. I was going to drown myself. I stared into oily black water from the height of several London bridges, but there were still a lot of people about and I had no wish to draw attention to myself. Then I thought, 'Why spoil my good new suit when there's a vital Government paper in the pocket?' So after a while I returned here. Don't worry, Arthur. The Report is in a perfectly safe place which nobody knows but me."

"More money. Is that what you want?"

"No. I want Ludmilla."

"You can't have her!" cried Shots.

"Then sod everything, Arthur," said McGrotty, and closed his eyes. Shots paced about the room in an agony of

---

* *Demotic Scotch for someone astonishingly self-assertive.*

exasperation. He said, "I can't *give* her to you, McGrotty!
She isn't mine."

"I know, Arthur," said McGrotty soothingly, "but you could
help me become the kind of man she's keen on — suave,
popular, the life and soul of Royal Garden Parties. Rich,
too, if that's any help. And quoted in the papers and on
television — I've always wanted to be quoted."

Shots sat down on the bedside and, with an effort, spoke
quietly again.

"Mungo. That letter. How can I explain? It's political
dynamite of the first water. I won't try to frighten you by
saying that, improperly used, it will mean the end of
civilisation. That's done for anyway, because we all find it
too inhibiting. I'll tell you this, however. If the information
in that document leaks out, every piece of money in the
world, every dollar, rouble, yen, pound sterling, credit-card
and cheque-book will become worthless paper. Do you
realise what this means?"

"I think so, Arthur. It means the Minister won't mind me
seeing a bit of Ludmilla now and then."

"For God's sake work *with* me, Mungo!" begged Arthur
Shots, "Only I have the *knowledge,* the *contacts,* the *finesse* to
handle something on this scale!"

Mungo nodded in agreement.

"Yes, I can see you'll be a lot of help to me, Uncle Arthur.
But first call on the Minister at ten sharp tomorrow when
he comes in for the Report. Tell him the score. Put him in
the picture. Ahoohay"—he yawned—"sorry I'm a bit tired.
I'll drop in before eleven and we'll work something out."

Shots stared at the can in his fist as if it was a vision of a
hideous future. He said, "In plain words, you are not simply
using the Report to blackmail the Minister, you are blackmailing *me* into blackmailing the Minister."

"That's right, Uncle Arthur!" said McGrotty, standing up. "And don't think you can't do it! You're the most persuasive talker I've heard!"

He went to the door and opened it in a way which showed their interview was over and all the time he chatted enthusiastically.
"That tongue of yours has had me doing things a kick from my Mammy's wellies wouldnae make me do. Never underrate yourself, Arthur. Areevaderchay, Arthur. You and me need a good night's sleep, Arthur. We've both had a tiring day."

17

"GOOD MORNING, MRS BEE!" THE Minister said, briskly entering his office. She said, "Good morning, sir. How did the opening go?" "Oh, very well. I'm fond of animals, even when they're stuffed, and a building in the middle had lots of that kind in it. Have you something special for me in the safe today?" "Yes, the Report from Mr Harbinger. I am sorry to hear he has shot himself."

"It was in all the papers," said the Minister gravely. "I too am sorry. He was a poor golfer, but they say he owned the finest collection of Florentine incunabula outside the British Museum. I always meant to ask him what incunabula were and now — too late! Never mind. At least he finished his Report. Fetch it, please."

He sat down at his desk like one sitting down to a state banquet. The occasion was a solemn one but he still expected to enjoy it. Mrs Bee laid an envelope before him stamped with the words EXTRA TOP SECRET AND CONFIDENTIAL beside a circle containing an image of the Crown Imperial. He slit the envelope with a paperknife and drew out a satisfyingly thick sheaf of foolscap. It took him two minutes of meticulous examination, three more minutes of frenzied re-examination, to see that every single sheet was blank. Even so he could not quite believe it. He was heartily relieved when Mrs Bee announced Sir Arthur Shots.

"Thank goodness you're here, Arthur!" he cried, pointing at the desktop littered with blank sheets. "Look what Harbinger sent me! No wonder he shot himself. He must have been off his chump."

"I can, er . . . explain how that happened, Bill," said Shots, clearing his throat. "The explanation will come as a shock, but when you've had time to absorb it you'll understand that matters could be much, much worse."

"What do you mean?"

"Two weeks ago you obliged Charlie Gold by taking a young Scot into this office."

"I really did it to oblige you. Charlie said McGrotty was a particular boy-friend of yours."

"Charlie told you that?" cried Shots indignantly. "And the bounder was my fag once. There's no loyalty nowadays. None! None!"

"Come to the point, Arthur."

"Well," said Shots mournfully, "I admit I once thought McGrotty was a clean potato but he's emerged as a rotten egg. He tells me he has stolen the Report and — er — hidden it."

After a long pause the Minister said, "Oh dear."

"Quite!" said Arthur Shots.

"We must put one of the Special Branches onto him," said the Minister, drumming his fingers.

"No. they would get back the Report all right, but what Special Branch officer could resist reading a document marked Extra Top Secret and Confidential? And then the Special Branch would be in a position to take over the running of the country."

"Are you sure of that?" cried the Minister.

"As sure as death."

"And does your friend McGrotty intend to take over the running of the country?"

"No, Bill. McGrotty's highest ambition is comparatively modest. He only wants . . . er . . . Ludmilla."

"Does he really believe he can make me prostitute my daughter by holding the country to ransom?" asked the Minister wildly. "He's as bad as the coalminers!"

"Not quite as bad, Bill! He only wants to meet her socially, to impress her with his prospects in life. I suggest we explain the matter to her and get her to wheedle the document out of him. She'll enjoy the Delilah bit."

"Haha, yes!" cried the Minister. "And then she'd read it and tell all her pals in the Women's Lib movement. We'd be giving her the power to plunge us all into a new dark age, and Ludmilla would never resist a temptation like that. The whole thing's a nightmare . . . By the way, Arthur, how are you involved?"

"Well, you see, Bill —" said Shots briskly, and paused.

"What happened, you see, was this —" said Shots more briskly still, and paused once more. At last he said lamely, "It's a very *complicated* story, Bill."

"Yes," said the Minister in a tired voice, "I see. I see very clearly that you, Arthur, are not just a bad hat. You are an *utter rotter.*"

"It takes all sorts to make a world, Bill," Shots pleaded, "I admit that I got you into this jam, so it is my responsibility to get you out. If you will only trust me a little I know I can manage it. What we must both do is —"

McGrotty entered without knocking.

18

NOT VULGARLY TRIUMPHANT, HIS manner was casual, with a hint of apology. He said, "Sorry to barge in, Bill, but has Arthur told you the score?"

The Minister stared at him, then nodded dumbly.

"So what do you suggest?"

After a long silence the Minister explained that he was having a small gathering in his home the following week: just the family and some intimate friends. Harbinger's death had reduced the guest list to thirteen. Drinks would be served at seven, dinner at eight.

"It'll be a start, socially," said McGrotty. "What about the career?"

"In three days' time," said the Minister with uncharacteristic force, "it will be announced in the *Times* that Arthur Shots, on grounds of age and ill-health, has resigned his post as head of the Criminal Disablement Department."

"Oh, steady on!" cried Shots.

"I shall offer the post to you, McGrotty."

"Thanks, Bill," said McGrotty.

"Now, Bill, you can't possibly —" said Shots.

"If you resist me in this, Arthur," said the Minister loudly, "I shall lay the whole matter in the lap of the P.M. She'll know how to handle you! I also expect you to resign from the National Repeal Club. I wish never to bump into you again."

"So be it, Bill," said Shots, "but you're making a mistake. I may be pretty foul but my kind of foulness does very little damage to things as they are, and in the long run I'm the only poison strong enough to keep down weeds like McGrotty here."

"Sticks and stones, Sir Shots," said McGrotty, "may break my bones, Sir Shots, but I am immune to nasty names."

Shots strolled to the door and turned.

"You mentioned the Prime Minister, Bill," he said pleasantly. "Were you more in touch with political facts you would know that as soon as she was told of Harbinger's suicide she at once ordered the Special Branch to bring all his papers to Downing Street. I doubt if she found much in them. Just now the Special Branch are questioning everyone who saw Harbinger yesterday, including his secretary and the external couriers. In a matter of minutes — not hours, but minutes — she will phone to demand the document Harbinger sent to you yesterday under conditions of elaborate precaution. Perhaps your new buddy will help you with that little problem. Meanwhile, I promise I cherish no hard feelings. I will be at your disposal when you approach me in the proper spirit."

The Minister's face went very pale. He chewed his fingers as Shots stepped from the room and softly shut the door behind him.

19

WHEN THE MINISTER CALMED DOWN he said, "McGrotty."

"Call me Mungo," said McGrotty.

"Mungo," said the Minister, "if the P.M. asks me for the Harbinger Report I will tell her the truth, for it is the only thing I know. All my life I have tried to be honest and I am a creature of habit. The truth I will tell her — that Harbinger insisted on sending his Report to my office instead of hers; that an employee in my office has stolen the Report; that he will not return it till he has seduced my daughter — this truth will make her think me a very clumsy liar who is plotting against her. This truth will destroy me politically, socially and (I fear) psychologically. But where is the lie which will make her think me honest?"

"On your desk!" said McGrotty eagerly, for he wanted to help his future father-in-law and hated the cruel way Shots had used him.

"My desk?"

"Put these blank pages back in the envelope," said McGrotty, "and phone her before she phones you.

Tell her exactly what you thought half an hour ago, before old Arthur said these nasty things to you. Say Harbinger sent you an envelope full of blank paper."

The Minister pondered. Yes, that story made sense. All Whitehall knew Harbinger had been brought to the verge of madness by a job which was too big for him. All Whitehall knew Harbinger had come to dread the outcome of his Report far more than those mentioned in it, for he was one and they were many. It was highly likely that he never wrote his Report or — having written it — faltered at the last moment, destroyed it, and posted blank sheets as a delaying tactic while summoning courage to kill himself. McGrotty, anxiously reading the Minister's tearfully cherubic features, saw the dawn of a childlike hope. McGrotty lifted the telephone and quietly told Mrs Bee that the Minister had urgent information he wished to convey to the P.M. by word of mouth. The Minister did not deny this but squared his shoulders, took a deep breath and accepted the receiver from McGrotty's hand.

"Prime Minister!" he said. "I must tell you I phoned Harbinger yesterday, to press for the Report, you know, and he spoke very oddly . . . You will check that? How can you . . . ? Oh, I see. Well, I'm glad the line was bugged because the tape will confirm that I . . ."

He spoke for five or six minutes, then put the phone down and dabbed his eyes with his handkerchief.

"She believed me!" he said with a small catch in his voice. "She even seemed relieved and oh, so am I. Forget what her enemies say, McGrotty, she is not a hard woman but tender-hearted, and in a quiet way truly religious. She called Harbinger a saint who had died for the sins of the Nation.

She said she had thought the Report a mere waste of time at first, as it could only contain information she would have to suppress, but the Special Branch have told her it was potentially more menacing than a hundred megaton nuclear warhead. 'With his own hands Harbinger seems to have dismantled the weapon we asked him to build,' she said to me, 'He destroyed the parts, the plans, and then himself, who alone knew how to build it. Harbinger died a martyr to the cause of the status quo!' she said. What fine sympathy she exhibited! What understanding! What power of language!"

"Harbinger did not destroy his Report," McGrotty reminded him.

The Minister closed his eyes and nodded his head spasmodically for a while.

"Quite so, McGrotty," he whispered at last, "and until it is destroyed — until you bring me that Report and burn every single page before my eyes (for I have no wish to read it) I will feel like a man living beneath the poised axe of a terrible giant."

"I'm not a giant," said McGrotty, offended, "I'm ordinary! I want nothing but a bit of respect and . . . and . . . to be quoted sometimes, and to marry the woman of my choice. These are not the desires of an extraterrestrial alien. When can I shift into Arthur's office? It has a very nice fireplace."

"Give him a day," said the Minister. "Meanwhile
please return to the outer office.
I now need solitude."

20

MRS BEE TOLD McGROTTY THE address of the Minister's town house on the edge of Hampstead Heath and told him that the Minister's wife lived apart from him. Ludmilla had a room in both parental homes but preferred her father's because she had more authority there.

McGrotty, arriving at exactly half past seven, was surprised to see a leading opposition politician and his wife arriving at the door in front of him. He had not known that in Britain leading political opponents entertain each other socially and are sometimes related. He was still more surprised to see neither of the two carried a bottle. Were the English upper classes so ill-mannered that they did not bring bottles to each other's parties? Should he hide in a flowerbed the very expensive bottle of champagne he carried? But a servant opened the door before he could do so. The servant helped remove the visitors' coats, and in removing McGrotty's took the bottle from him. "That bottle is a present for your boss," explained McGrotty.

"I see, sir," said the servant, and returned the bottle, so McGrotty had to carry it into a crowded drawing room.

"Oh, there you are," said the Minister, smiling crookedly at someone behind McGrotty's left shoulder.

"Hullo, Bill. This is a nice big house, Bill. Here is my contribution to the current jollifications, Bill."

"Very good. Excuse me," said the Minister, and moved away. There was no visible drink buffet but two servants carried round little trays loaded with glasses of sherry, whisky and orange. McGrotty crammed the magnum onto one of these trays then moved toward the sharp, clear, crystalline voice of Ludmilla. It came from behind a burly man with an American voice who spoke of his Pop Panic exhibition at the South Bank.

"I want to hear all about that," said Ludmilla greedily.

"Hullo, Ludmilla!" said McGrotty.

"We take the public upstairs in an old-fashioned ghost train," said the artist, "and they come out in an open space where . . . broom-baroom . . . four Hell's Angels on motor-bikes come riding round them in a ring that gets smaller and smaller till they have to escape by jumping down a hole in the floor."

"What a fantastic mind you have!" said Ludmilla. "Where does this hole take them?"

"Down a chute to the exit."

"This is a nice big room, Ludmilla," said McGrotty.

"What if someone has a heart attack?" asked Ludmilla.

"Your Arts Council will pay for the damage."

McGrotty wandered away with that severe pain in the diaphragm which a minute of Ludmilla's company always gave him.

"Hello!" said a pleasant and beautiful old lady, "You look rather out of things. So am I, in a way. Let me introduce myself. I'm Mary Fox. Dame Mary Fox. I am an actress."

"I don't go to pantomimes," said McGrotty bitterly.

"I'm not surprised, nowadays. Are you in Bill's Ministry?"

"Head of Criminal Disablement."

"Ah! Then I have a bone to pick with you. I am part-time secretary of a charitable foundation called Kleptomaniacs Anonymous. Why won't your department answer our letters?"

"New to the job, excuse me," said McGrotty. He lunged towards a tray, grabbed a glass, poured the contents straight over his thrapple and at once regretted it. Spirits were indeed bad for his head, which he felt rotating on its axis. He knew this was an illusion and managed not to stagger, but even worse was the self-pity which suddenly flooded him. "I am lonely," he thought, "I have always been lonely." The self-pity became murderous rage. Only he knew the whereabouts of a Report more menacing than a hundred megaton nuclear warhead, yet everyone here either ignored him or condescended to him. Charlie Gold said, "Hello, Mungo. Reaping the fruits of your enterprise?"

"PLUCKING!" shouted McGrotty, so loudly that everyone else fell silent.

"I beg your pardon?"

"Fruit is plucked, not reaped."

"Dinner seems to be ready now," announced the Minister in a voice which also sounded desperately loud. "Shall we go through?"

In the dining room he was placated, at first, to find his chair beside Ludmilla's. He said, "I'm glad I'm sitting beside you, Ludmilla."

She said, "You've someone on your other side too, and so, thank God, have I."

Mary Fox said brightly, "We meet again, Mr — I'm sorry, I haven't caught your name."

"Oh, hullo there," said McGrotty, and glumly prodded with a fork the content of a glass dish on the table before him. Below a thick cream he discovered plump little articulated bodies. "What are these beetles doing in my horse dewars?" he asked, aghast.

"They aren't beetles, they're prawns," explained Mary Fox.

"I'm not eating muck like this!" cried McGrotty. "Hey, Ludmilla! These are very nice knives and forks, Ludmilla! They're a queer shape but I like them a lot, Ludmilla!"

"How am I supposed to reply to that?" said Ludmilla distinctly in the ensuing silence.

"You talk as if I was keech*," yelled McGrotty, "the only keech in the room! Well, I have proof to the contrary! *Documentary* proof that some people here are a load of worse keech than I am!"

"Come with me!" said Ludmilla through gritted teeth. She stood up, gripped his sleeve and pulled him from the room.

"A rough diamond, but brilliant in his field of course," said the Minister brokenly as she slammed the door behind her.

---

* Keech: *excrement, Scottish. The final* ch *is hard, as in Bach.*

21

LUDMILLA LED HIM QUICKLY THROUGH several rooms and into a small tropical garden protected by glass walls and a dome. An ornate cast-iron bench with thin cushions stood in the centre.

"Sit down and cool off," said Ludmilla, sitting down and folding her arms. He sat beside her. He felt perfectly sober now, and delighted to have exactly the companion he wanted.

"Well now!" he said brightly. "What shall we talk about?"

"We have nothing to talk about. You have just ruined a rather enjoyable dinner party."

"Aren't you curious about my hold over your Daddy?"

"Not at all. It probably has to do with the asphalt shares he picked up when he was Secretary for Motorways. I'm *bored* by this sordid politicking!" she said violently.

"Animals then?"

"What do you know about animals?"

"When I was eleven I taught a mouse to waltz," said Mungo smugly.

"Nonsense. How could you?"

"I played him tunes on my mouth-organ at mealtimes and made him stand up and beg for his cheese and sugar. Eventually he waltzed in circles whenever he heard the music."

"Pavlov did that sort of thing to dogs," Ludmilla said, grinding her teeth again. "And Pavlov was a bastard."

"But it wasnae like that with me, Ludmilla!" cried McGrotty. "Wee Jimmy got to like waltzing. He would do it between meals, round and round the kitchen table. The other kids paid me twopence a skull just to see him. Then"—he sighed—"then one day he waltzed too far. He fell off the table. The cat got him."

"Oh, poor little chap!"

"Jimmy was my first and last pet," he told her solemnly.

"You see, Mungo," she said quite kindly, "animals take naturally to some human activities — like horses to foxhunting — but no animal should ever be asked to stand on its hind legs. Promise not to do that again."

"I promise. Ludmilla, I am not an idiot. I know I behaved disgustingly tonight. I've got no savwar fare, Ludmilla, but . . . I'm a fast learner! Listen, I don't want to interfere with your social life, but surely you could spare me a few afternoons? Show me the sights. Teach me the moves," he pleaded. "Tell me what to wear."

She asked stonily, "What will I get out of it?"

"I might tell your Daddy's secret. It's actually more interesting than asphalt shares. Go on — give me one afternoon."

"Tomorrow."

"Tomorrow?"

"I want," she explained, "to get it over as quickly as possible."

He sighed, stood up and said quietly, "Goodnight. I'm going home. Tell your Dad not to worry. I'm sorry I acted like that, and I'm not going to any more parties for a long, long time."

She was taken aback by the dignity of his manner but pleased to get rid of him before the evening had been totally ruined. She said, "Can you find your own way out?"

"Don't worry," he said, departing, "I've a good memory."

But before her evening ended Ludmilla was called to the telephone.

"Ludmilla!" said a guarded voice. "Arthur speaking."

"Uncle Arthur!" she said gaily, because she had always found him entertaining. "I've been reading in *The Times* how old and sick you are."

"Yes, I'm in a jam. So's your father. And you know who's to blame, don't you?"

"I did notice Daddy's even more flustered than usual. But he keeps muttering about you."

"Ha! Blames me, does he? Well, I'm not surprised. He's in the claws of the most Machiavellian snake in London."

"How exciting!"

"Listen, Ludmilla, I'm convinced that you alone can save us. Your father doesn't agree with me, but I know you can save us. Because you're British. Yes, the little girl I used to dandle is British to the core."

She giggled. Arthur always appealed to patriotic sentiment when he was in a mess. She arranged to meet him next morning.

22

"COME IN HERE AND SEE ME, PYTHON," said McGrotty to the intercom of his new office. "My name is *Panther*, Mr McGrotty."
"Come in all the same."

He was sitting in exactly the corner of the sofa which Arthur Shots had preferred, and it occurred to her that if Shots had not taken his smoking jacket away McGrotty would have been wearing it. He watched her closely for a while, rubbing his chin, then said, "Is a beard a good idea? For me, I mean."
"Yes, Mr McGrotty."
"But won't I look a bit of a ruffian while I'm growing it?"
"I doubt if the difference will be widely noted, Mr McGrotty."
"Wit!" said McGrotty without smiling. "A distinct wee joke. I'm glad you too are a bit of a clown, Python. Well, a beard it shall be. How long have you had this job?"
"Twelve years, Mr McGrotty."
"So you understand the department better than anyone?"
"Quite so, Mr McGrotty."

"Then I'm leaving the work to you. I know I'll have to sign papers, and attend the odd meeting, but you'll tell me when and how. Right?"

"It's the usual arrangement, though seldom stated so clearly, Mr McGrotty."

He stood up and paced about with hands clasped behind his back.

"Understand, Miss Python, that I do not plan to be a mere cipher, a chancer, a no-user. Tomorrow you will tell me what Criminal Disablement is and why folk need it, but not today. Today I will tell you about me, Miss Python. The ignorant majority see me as the dour, hard practical Scot of legend, and of course I am that, basically; but I am also a man of passions, and even instincts. Mistake me not! I am no mad rapist, but this afternoon I wish to transact some private business with nothing in mind but my own personal satisfaction. Can you get me a suitable typist? An intelligent widow of thirty-five, say, or an empty-headed but ambitious wee lassie of eighteen? Even you, Miss Python, are not, in my estimation, devoid of charm, though of course I am not pressing you."

Miss Panther closed her eyes, wishing her nerves would allow her the luxury of swooning. Her pride in life was to be a perfect instrument in the hands of highly placed men, an instrument of such excellent quality that the men using her felt comparatively cheap. Arthur Shots had been the only chief whose qualities (she felt) nearly matched her own. Mungo McGrotty made her feel that the role she had chosen in life was perhaps a tragic one. She opened her eyes and said faintly, "I can provide you with a suitable typist."

"Good girl, Python!" he said. "See to it. And I'll try to find a fiddle for raising your wages. I haven't discovered the limits of my powers yet. Perhaps tomorrow you will advise me on them. But Arthur Shots offered to put my name in the honours list, so I suppose I can do the same for you, if you're keen."

She said, "Thank you, Mr McGrotty," and left.

McGrotty continued to pace the room, brooding and sighing to himself. His dream of marrying Ludmilla had been destroyed the night before. Nothing remained for him but the gloomy consolations of power. The telephone rang. Miss Panther said, "The Minister's daughter is here, Mr McGrotty. She says she has an appointment."

"Eh? Oh."

"I shall send her in and will retard the typist."

"Good girl, Python."

23

LUDMILLA HAD CHOSEN TO BE EXOTIC in an outdoor way that afternoon. She wore a riding habit with boots, breeches and jockey cap; her hair hung in two schoolgirl plaits; her makeup suggested she wore none at all but had just dismounted after a brisk gallop. She stood near the door, giving him time to appreciate the pink flush, shining black and bottle green of her, but he was not impressionable today. He merely rubbed his chin and looked. At last she said brightly, "Mungo!"

He said warily, "What do you want, Ludmilla?"

"Hadn't I arranged to go out with you today?"

"No."

For a thoughtful moment she tapped the side of her boot with her crop then said, "The truth is, I've been brooding about you, and I've begun to think you may not be the wholesale disaster I assumed."

"Go on."

"You see you can't help shambling and slouching so ordinary good tailoring looks second-hand on you. But designer gear would be even worse, because it has a joi-de-vivre quality that your whole manner contradicts. What you need are shaggy tweeds: the best quality of course, and tremendously well cut in something like the style of an Edwardian gamekeeper. That would make you look quite sexy in a Hunchback-of-Notre-Dame way."

"Ludmilla!" he cried, awed by her insight. "My grandfather was a gillie on the Earl of Home's estate!"

"There you are!" she said triumphantly.

"Ludmilla, I'm going to telephone my tailor and tell him lies and bluster and threaten and bribe till he agrees to see me within the hour. And you'll come too and give him the orders, right?"

"Right!"

"And in return I want to buy clothes for you: a complete outfit of the most devastating, expensive — expensively glamorous"—he pulled himself together—"in fact, a complete outfit, but I want to see you choose it."

"It'll cost you a packet if you do that!" she grinned wickedly.

"A dawdle! A dawdle!*" he boasted.

"A dawdle?"

"I will not join those herds who reinvest their surplus just to make it even bigger. I will encourage the workers by purchasing the finest products of their toil and donating it to — to — to someone who likes — who pretends to like me." His humility came as a relief. She said frankly,

---

* *The English verb dawdle means to waste time, be sluggish or loiter, but in Scotland it is also used as a noun for a short, easy stroll, and has acquired a third meaning through its application to the sport of Association Football. The admirers of a player who has achieved a goal in difficult circumstances sometimes call his achievement a dawdle, meaning "For someone of his unusual powers the thing was easy." McGrotty is employing the word in this third, distinctly vainglorious sense.*

"That's a very sensible attitude. I think I can give you exactly what you want without pretending a thing. Fix me a gin and tonic and phone your tailor. No, just phone. I'll get the drink myself."

She knew the office well. The contents of the cocktail cabinet had not been touched since Arthur Shots moved out, though several cans of Younger's Tartan Special had been added. As they left the office she slid an arm through his and said, "I've a studio just off Bond Street. We can go there after our shopping and I'll run us up a little snack."
"I didn't know you were an artist!"
"I'm not, but a studio always comes in handy. An uncle gave me this one for my birthday."

24

THE STUDIO JUST OFF BOND STREET had an inconspicuous little door between a commercial art gallery and a video rental agency. The door opened on steep stairs not much wider than McGrotty's shoulders, stairs that went straight up without landings for a very long way. They ended in the corner of a room eight feet square. The only studio feature was the ceiling, a skylight with nothing above it but the sky. A circular bed with black quilt, sheets and pillow almost touched each wall. A corner had a dressing table with makeup and a vibrator on it, another held a neat structure containing a television set, record player and tape collection. Ludmilla dropped her shopping bags, threw off her cap and jacket then slotted in a silent video film of multiracial couples coupling. She said, "Choose some music. Make yourself comfortable," and entered the kitchen, which was the size of a cupboard but intricately equipped. McGrotty's favourite music was from the soundtrack of films. He put on the theme from *Chariots of Fire,* decided to sit on the bed and found the mattress was stuffed with water. He could not sit on it comfortably so took off his shoes and lay flat. The shopping had excited him. Squandering of wealth upon mere appearance — wealth which could have fed, housed and healed people — had given him an erection at times. He had not believed before that waste could be enjoyed for its own sake. He kept reminding himself that the two thousand pounds he had spent on Ludmilla was only a tenth of his monthly salary after taxation. But now melancholy mingled with excitement. He knew he would soon enjoy all he desired, that the enjoyment would be brief and would be paid for with more than money. He gave a heartfelt sigh.

"Cheer up!" said Ludmilla, laying a tray on the bed. It held rye-bread slices covered with tasty lumps and smears, a champagne bottle and two glasses. She removed her boots and blouse, sat beside him and opened the bottle. It popped, smoked, then fizzed into the glasses. She did not spill a drop.

"Use it to wash down this," she ordered, handing him a pill from an unlabelled bottle on the dressing table.

"Why? What is it? What will it do?"

"Trust me and take it."

"Why don't you take one?"

"I don't need one, but to allay your fears, alright, I will."

They swallowed their pills, sipped and nibbled. McGrotty began to feel wonderfully contented and pleased with himself, as helplessly pleased and contented as a baby, then the helpless feeling was replaced by a sensation of strength, a sensation so great that he felt able to grasp everything he wanted.

"Careful!" said Ludmilla, wincing. "Don't charge at it."

She shifted the tray to the floor.

Like most people who find sex more of an amusement than a passion Ludmilla was not very sensual, but could please men when she wanted to. That day it amused her to discover how much pleasure she could give McGrotty without letting him enter her. He took more pleasure than she had thought possible, reacting so extravagantly that several times she burst out laughing. So did he, eventually. She kissed him and murmured, "Mmmungo, you asked me to come out with you today. I can't go further out with you than this."

"Yes, you can."

"But I won't. Where have you hidden the Report, Mmmungo?"

"You'll have to seduce me thoroughly before I tell you that. All my life I have dreamed of being thoroughly seduced by a lovely, cold-hearted and utterly depraved, upper-class English girl."

"You scheming little rat!" she said, with a touch of admiration.

"You like animals."

"Not rats."

"In that case," said McGrotty, and roaring like a lion he turned her over and, like a lion, mounted and penetrated her.

Afterwards she wakened him with another kiss and said, "Where exactly is it, Mmmungo?"

"In your Daddy's safe," he said dreamily.

"What?"

"There is a very big old iron tray in the safe. I pushed the envelope underneath it."

She sat up and stared at him. "You only pretended to steal it?"

"Yes."

"That's brilliant!"

"No. Spur of the moment. I suppose," he said as the first wave of misery hit him, "I suppose you've finished with me now."

"I'm not . . . entirely sure," she said.

The phone rang.

25

THE PHONE WAS CORDLESS. McGROTTY had not seen it under the pillow. Ludmilla lifted it. "Poco presto!" whispered Arthur Shots. It was his password.

Ludmilla stood up saying, "A sugar-daddy wants to whisper sweet nothings to me so I'm going where you can't hear us, Mungo."

She stepped into the kitchen, shut the door and murmured, "Arthur. In Daddy's safe is an antique tray full of rubber stamps which haven't been used since the Boer War. He pushed the Report under the tray. It's still there."

"But . . . that's clever!"

"Yes, he must be smart to have outwitted Daddy and you."

"Of course! Ludmilla, I'm sorry the Report is in your father's safe."

"Why?"

"Because it's full of delicious filth about all kinds of top people, filth the goverment won't let us know about for a million years."

"Oh, Daddy's sure to give me a peep. After all, I found it for him."

"You'll be disappointed, Ludmilla. Your father's terrified of you reading the Report. That's why he's never let you know it existed. So now we'll never learn why the Pope had poor Kennedy shot."

"How bloody unfair!"

"I agree," he said, then kept silent, leaving her mind to tackle the problem.

A second later she said, "Arthur, I sometimes leave my shopping in that safe when I'm in town. I'll leave some there tomorrow morning and call for it after lunch. Have your car outside the Ministry at two thirty sharp."

"I will!" he said gladly. "And then we'll zoom off to our little love nest and, oh, Ludmilla, what an afternoon we'll have!"

"Two thirty sharp Arthur," she said and returned, brooding, to the room.

The sight of McGrotty standing half dressed beside the bed perplexed her for a moment. She had forgotten him. She said, "Please hurry, I've to dress for a dinner engagement. I can't concentrate on that with a man around my feet."

26

AND AT TWO THIRTY SHOTS' NEAT little sedan two-seater arrived at the kerb in front of the Ministry. He left the engine running, opened the window on the pavement side and leaned across the passenger seat, staring out. A minute later Ludmilla emerged and crossed the pavement. She nodded and showed him the corner of an envelope in her shopping bag. He said, "Splendid! Hop in."

"I . . . can't. The door's locked."

"No, just jammed. Give me the Report, put down your bag and use both hands."

She did these things.

He pressed the switch which automatically closed the window then drove swiftly away, leaving her screaming after him like a fury out of Hell. He sincerely regretted cheating Ludmilla but his grand design had no place in it for an equal partner.

27

RTHUR SHOTS DROVE TO HIS home in Kingston-upon-Thames, told his house-keeper to tell all callers he was out, and locked himself with the Report in his study. He began reading it in a mood of jubilant elation. Two hours later, having read it three times, he was a gravely anxious man.

He had thought he knew at least half the contents of the Report, since he himself had given Harbinger some very deadly information. He discovered that he had not known a hundredth part of all the Report contained. Harbinger had correlated his own information with news from Trade and Industry, Fuel and Power, Transport, the Atomic Energy Commission, the Exchequer, the Home Office, the Foreign Office, the Armed Services, the Security Services and the Inland Revenue. Each unit of information was, in a quiet way, shocking, but all of them fitted into something like (he shuddered at the notion) a horrible huge, living-but-disembodied hand which gripped the throat of all Britain. The first half of the Report anatomised this hand, named the bones, joints and tendons, and explained how they worked together. (He was interested to see that he himself corresponded to the abductor muscle of the thumb.)

The second half of the Report went further. With a skilled surgeon's eye for detailed connection, Harbinger had deduced the body of which this hand was only part, the body of a beast which pressed on the world. With the intuitive logic of a clear-brained scholar he had named the parts of this body also and outlined the nervous system, guts and bloodstream. (Shots shuddered again. He had been thinking metaphorically, but his metaphor reminded him of a page in the Report which described new and disturbing uses of human blood.) Harbinger — this mild, unambitious humane hobbyist — emerged in his Report as something of a genius. In a few pages of distinct manuscript he had described the whole nature of the beast and had then sanely and conscientiously shot himself. This no longer seemed the act of a madman. The beast was too huge to be opposed and in the near future would grow insupportably vaster. No sane man would wish to share the world with it — unless he was riding on top of it. Arthur Shots emitted a little whimper of excitement. He had promoted the notion of the Report and secretly leaked information against himself in order to raise cabinet backing for it. He had thought he was forging a chain to bind the nation. He now held a chain to bind the planet, or (to put the case in a different way) the world was everywhere in chains: the Report was potentially a chain to bind the chainers, if he could slip the links round their limbs with sufficient dexterity.

"Aye, there's the rub!" he exclaimed. "I know I have the dexterity, but have I the strength? The strength I must expend for several crucial years will verge on the superhuman. If I make but one slip the best I can hope for is a mercifully quick death by an assassin's bullet. He either fears his fate too much or his desserts are small. That puts it not unto the touch to win or lose it all, but — I am no longer young. Thank God only three others know the Report. These three must die, when I have attained the power. Yes, yes, even Ludmilla, the only woman I ever loved — the only girl able to satisfy my sexual appetites after she passed the age of twelve — she too must die along with the execrable McGrotty."

He shed tears and took a brandy to steady himself. "All power ennobles!" he announced. "And absolute power ennobles absolutely, but the strong are lonely. That will be my tragedy. The world will not guess it till many centuries have elapsed. But one day the Shakespeares, the Tolstoys, the Verdis of an unborn age will make my agony the subject of their highest art. Ludmilla must die. But not at once. Just now, gentler methods will suffice. She is but a woman. I will dose her with a strong compound of bribes and flattery. Her father can be cowed by a single well-directed threat. McGrotty (ha ha ha ha ha ha, how I shall enjoy it) McGrotty will be silenced by a protracted regime of unrelenting mental agony."

This thought dispelled his gloom for a while. He arranged the details in his mind, then attended to calls which had collected in his answer phone. Most of them were from the Minister, brokenly asking for an interview. Ludmilla had clearly told him the news. Shots phoned the Minister and said, "Poco presto."

"Arthur," babbled the Minister, "Arthur, about the —"

"Don't say it," said Shots.

"No! Wild horses won't drag that word from my lips. But please give me that — thing."

"Come and talk to me about it. Tonight. Now."

"Must I?"

"Yes. How's Ludmilla?"

"Still smashing things in her room."

"Poor kid!" said Shots with real sympathy. "Tell her I'll pay
for the damage."

28

McGROTTY TOOK A DAY OFF work to recover from his afternoon with Ludmilla. It had been the greatest time of his life, how could he live after it? How could he live without it? How could it not have been the greatest time in Ludmilla's life? But he knew it had not been. The brief puzzled look she gave him when she returned from phoning in the kitchen showed he had vanished from her mind as soon as he gave up his secret. He lay on his hostel bed (it had not occurred to him to seek brighter lodgings) and recalled all of yesterday again and again, starting with Python's announcement of Ludmilla's arrival, passing through all the deliriums of shopping and sexuality, and ending with that little glance which showed all was over. Through the hours of daylight that remembered glance pierced his heart again and again, and through the sleepless hours of night it slowly hardened him. Next morning he got up determined to grasp once more the consolations of mere power, little though he valued them.

He entered the outer office feeling and looking shabbier than ever before. His facial hair was now a distinct beard, but ragged and entangled. Seeing Miss Panther, he decided to fish for sympathy. He hitched a thigh and buttock onto a corner of her desk and asked, "Ever been disappointed in love, Python?"

"My name is Panther."

"I asked you a question, Panther."

"I have never been disappointed in love."

He brooded on this reply then decided for rhetorical reasons to ignore it. He said, "Have you ever had all your wildest dreams come blindingly true and then phut! Nothing? You were left clutching but a handful of withered memories?"

After a pause Miss Panther asked distinctly, "Do you wish me to dredge you something from the typing pool?"

He was shocked. He said, "Python! Python! What has got into you? That is not the remark of a perfect secretary! Sex is no cure for a bleeding heart, Python. Work is the cure. Hard work. I am going to make Criminal Disablement the strongest department of the Ministry of Social Stability. I am going to give Social Stability huge sharp jaggy teeth and claws, Miss Python. So send the mail through to my office, and a nice cup of tea, and see if you can get me a pocket-sized vernacular translation of *Mein Kampf*—"

He stopped because he had strolled to the door of the inner office, opened it and entered.

Arthur Shots, in braided smoking jacket,
sat in his usual corner of the leather settee.

29

"COME IN, MUNGO MY BOY," SAID Shots quietly, and stood up, "No, you are not dreaming. I am back in my rightful place. I did not need to see you this morning but it was a luxury I could not refuse myself."

"Arthur," said McGrotty.

"You are too sentimental for a political careerist, McGrotty. Your little spell of giddy power ended two days ago in your orgy with Ludmilla. You were fool enough to trust a woman, McGrotty!" said Shots, and laughed.

"But I didn't trust her!" McGrotty protested. "I told her where the Report was because she'd been nice to me."

"Petit bourgeois poppycock!" shouted Shots. "I had you promoted, McGrotty, because I believed that, though stupid, ill-mannered, and badly dressed, you were capable of the unfashionable virtue of *loyalty*. But you have bitten the hand of the goose that laid the golden eggs and I am going to make you squirm. There are more than twenty special branches of her Majesty's secret security service and I am going to have you investigated by every one of them — in rotation."

"But there's nothing! I mean, nothing for them to, nothing to —" said McGrotty.

"Nothing for them to discover. Exactly! But *they* won't know that. Just think! For the rest of your life every employer who gives you a job, every landlord of every dwelling you try to hide in, every man, woman and child who is fool enough to befriend you will be visited and questioned by sinister officials with the full backing of the British Goverment. They will be pestered again and again for details of your finances, feeding habits and sex-life. How long do you think you'll be able to last, McGrotty?"

McGrotty tugged his beard. He said, "Can I do anything to make amends, Sir Arthur?"

"Yes, indeed!" said Shots gleefully. "Don't kill yourself! I want you to live many miserable years of friendless, homeless penury, I want you to breathe your last on the ripped upholstery of a provincial social security office, and don't think you can escape me by defecting to Sweden! Before you reached the airport you would be whisked into the sound-proof ward of a suburban nursing-home and there you would learn that brain-washing is no *picnic*, Mungo McGrotty!"

"Sir Shots!" said McGrotty with dignity. "You are not just trying to depress me. You are being deliberately unkind."

"Clear out!" yelled Shots. "Clear out! Clear out! Clear out — !"

He did not stop yelling until he fell backward, coughing, into his corner of the sofa.

He wondered what demonic force in McGrotty had made him lose control of himself and spoil a perfectly fair piece of private vengeance. But the force unhinging him was not in McGrotty.

It was in the Report.

30

H E TRUDGED FROM THE MINISTRY, miserable and dazed. It was logical that the downward slide which began when Ludmilla rejected him should continue till he died. He hardly bothered to moan when two harsh hands grasped his sleeve, painfully nipping the arm inside. He thought it was the police and felt relieved.

"Mungo!" said an angry voice. "Where do you think you're going, you *utter fool!*"

But the face was Ludmilla's, glaring and grinding its teeth. This was worse than the police. With a cry he tried to pull away but she kept tight hold. They were on the Ministry steps. Twisting his arm behind his back, she marched him up the pavement and past the Cenotaph. He said, "Leave me alone, Ludmilla."

"You stupid, stupid idiot!" she hissed. "Why didn't you warn me against Arthur Shots? Why didn't you tell me *everything?*"

"Leave me alone!"

"Oh no, you aren't going to escape as easily as that."

"I told you what you asked me to tell you, I thought you knew everything else. Oh, don't be nasty to me!" he wept.

"Stop snivelling."

"I cannae *help* it! I don't care when other people are nasty to me because I don't like them. But you were nicer to me the day before yesterday than even my Mammy is and I can't bear it! I can't! *Can't!* WON'T!" he shouted, getting angry.

"Pull yourself together!" she said, releasing him and confronting him with her fists on her hips. "It is utterly pointless getting emotional before we've worked out what to do."

"We?" he asked, in a new tone.

She took a comb from her handbag and gave it to him.

"Use that on your head and face and we'll go to a quiet little tearoom I know near Charing Cross. Try to look less like some wino I've picked up. Compassion for underdogs went out with Jesus Christ and John Lennon."

The tearoom was below pavement level and devoid of other customers at that early hour. Ludmilla ordered two very strong sweet Turkish coffees then said, "You're desperate, I hope?"

"Oh yeah!"

"Good, then you'll do something. Daddy isn't desperate, he's just hopeless. Arthur is taking the Report to the Palace this afternoon."

"*THE PALACE?????*"

"Yes. Have you forgotten Britain is a Monarchy? And the Queen is Arthur's cousin. Anyway, the Queen will then summon the Prime Minister to the Palace and the Prime Minister will resign for reasons of health, but not before announcing the date of a general election. After that Arthur will stand for parliament in a good safe Tory seat, poor old

Dad will be kicked into the House of Lords and *Arthur*, bloody *Arthur*, will become the new Social Stability Minister. And that, for Arthur, is just the beginning! Dad keeps mooning around the house moaning that Arthur's too clever for him. Arthur isn't really clever. He just has an unusual quantity of the cunning of his breed."

"What breed is that?" asked McGrotty, who knew only two breeds of folk: himself and the others.

"The political breed. You see there are political people and financial people and animal people and art people. I'm animal with a smattering of art, actually, but it's recently struck me that politics could be fun if treated like a blood sport. You haven't any breeding of course. You're nothing." She blew a smoke-ring.

"Nothing?" said McGrotty, startled, because he was sure he existed.

"You belong to the class who have to take the first job they can get. With a bit of extra push you could become anything" —she frowned thoughtfully—"anything at all."

McGrotty said glumly, "We'll never get that Report back from Arthur."

"Our only hope is to find out what it says. There must be *somebody* who knows."

"Oh, I know what it says," said McGrotty off-handly.

She stared at him. "How can you?"

"I was hanging around your Dad's office for a couple of days while Arthur moved out of his. Nobody knew there was anything in the safe but the ordinary secret papers, so I was able to take out the Report for something to read when I went to the lavatory. There were some rare laughs in it."

"What does it say?"

He sighed and told her it involved the Mafia, the World Monetary Fund, a European Necrophilia ring and the CIA — not the American CIA but the Chinese CIA. The American CIA was also in it, but did not know it was in it. The link was a prominent member of the British cabinet.

"Not *Daddy?*" asked Ludmilla, thrilled.

He shook his head, whispered a name, and said, "But without the Report who will believe a thing like that? The astonishing fact is, that hardly any member of this —" he hesitated.

"Conspiracy?" she suggested.

"But it's not a conspiracy, or not like the conspiracies in the James Bond film with one evil mastermind. Hardly anyone in this — let's call it an organisation — knows all the organisations that are part of it. The few who understand most of it are so widely scattered that they never meet on a personal level. They have only one thing in common."

His voice became a very quiet whisper indeed, but her hearing was perfect.

"Eternal life!" she said.

"Yes."

"And some heads of state are getting this stuff?"

"Isn't it obvious?"

"How bloody unfair! We must get some."

"But you see," said McGrotty, "It's made by —" He talked very quietly again. Ludmilla was greatly excited by the information which had made Harbinger kill himself and was driving Shots into premature senile dementia.

She said jubilantly, "We did not make the world, Mungo. We must take it as we find it and do the best we can. Are you able to type that out exactly as you've told it to me?"

"A dawdle. Folk seem to think I kept getting decent transfers because I'm an idiot. Actually it's because I've a filing-cabinet memory. I can remember everything I've ever read, word for word, if it's official. What's wrong with you?"

Ludmilla was staring at him with an odd expression. She had gone pale. "Mungo!" she said faintly. "I believe I need you to touch me. You give me dizzy feelings of power. You know so much and you're such putty."

He blushed and shrugged.

31

SHE TOOK HIM TO HER APARTMENT on Park Lane. It was a present from a great and good young author who had also installed a word processor under the illusion that his generosity would induce her to type his novels, but the only literary habit Ludmilla had ever learned was dictation. McGrotty sat down and in two hours typed a verbatim transcript of the whole Report.

They printed out several copies, phoned for a taxi and went to see Ludmilla's father.

32

S IR ARTHUR, ON HIS COMFORTABLE
sofa, sat with a glass of brandy in one hand, the
Report on his knees and an open metal briefcase
beside him. He was reading the Report for the last time
before the car arrived to take him to the Palace. The Report
still had power to astonish him. The coming interview with
his cousin was a crucial one, but it would not tax him
mentally. He was glad of this for he felt feverish. He had
also overheard himself talking quite loudly in blank verse
when he thought he was alone. Dangerous! And he
suspected he was drinking more than usual. Tomorrow he
would start cutting down the alcohol: just now he would
have one last large brandy for the road. He laid the Report
in the case and went to his global cabinet, but instead of
opening it he first soothed himself by massaging the
continents with his palms, murmuring, "Oh cruel fate, to
grant me all I ask When I am in my sixties and have come
Unto the very doorstep of the tomb! Eternal life!
Perhaps! But who will be Eternalised is one no longer
young. Even my gout will be eternalised, Besides my vivid
qualities of mind. Oh were I now that brisk young

rugger Blue, That Blue who ravished Oxford in his prime, I might have, in a century or two, shown to the swarming millions of this globe The Adoniac outlines of my form, And they'd have loved me as the God I am! But am, alas, at heart, only at heart."

He sighed, poured another stiff brandy and muttered, "I must control all from *behind* the scenes, Clothed as a drab Prime Minister of State. Oh is there nowhere someone I can find To see, know, love and help me as I am? I wish you were less *greedy* Ludmilla, Less of a scheming, selfish little bitch. You could have been the Yin unto my Yang, Vice to my versa, Hera to my Zeus. You could have been my helpmate and my friend, But you are greedy, and so there's an end."

The phone rang. Miss Panther said quietly, "May I see you for a moment, Sir Arthur?"

"Why yes! Why not?"

Miss Panther entered, closing the door carefully behind her. She said, "The Minister's daughter is in the outer office with her father and Mungo McGrotty."

"Indeed!"

"I told them you could see nobody just now, that you were about to attend an absolutely essential appointment."

"Good."

"The Minister's daughter said you would change your mind if I mentioned just one word to you, Sir Arthur."

"Word?" said Shots, puzzled. "What word?"

"I believe it was . . . pantocratoraphorbia."

Shots dropped his glass, which smashed.

"*Panto — ?*" he whispered.

"cratorapho —"

"No! No! Don't say it! Please don't ever say that word!" he pled. "You don't know what it means!" He writhed like a

man to whom all thought has suddenly become a kind of
torture.

"Do you then intend to see these visitors, Sir Arthur?"

Shaking head in wild denial, he whimpered, "Yes."

"Shall I put Her Majesty off, Sir Arthur?"

Nodding head in wild assent, he whimpered, "No."

She left, and sent the visitors in.

33

THE MINISTER LOOKED HALF STUNNED so Shots knew at once he must have read the Report. Shots knew wrong. The Minister had refused to read more than the first half-page. McGrotty was now so unlike the despicable hobo who had strolled into that room seven hours before that Shots felt his grip on reality loosen yet further. McGrotty's hair and beard were now expertly trimmed. He wore a suit and waistcoat of golden brown Harris tweed cut in a conventional but out-of-date style, and though not made to measure it seemed to fit him perfectly. This was because he stood erect and did so — not like a drill sergeant, as if trained to it — but easily, like one who, in a quiet way, has achieved a good place in the world. His trustworthy appearance was enhanced by a folder of papers he carried. This gave him the aspect of an old-fashioned but dependable friend of the family, some doctor or solicitor who had risen by his own efforts from the ranks of the working classes and was all the better for it, as he could never be corrupted by the luxuries of the rich. This aspect of McGrotty is well known to the reader — he kept it when he stood for Parliament. But the change that chilled

Shots most was in Ludmilla. She wore flat-soled shoes, sensible slacks and a sweater. She had been working too hard on McGrotty's appearance to care about her own, and when Shots saw this he knew she had defeated him. She said, "Sit down and stop shuddering, Arthur, we mean to be quite kind to you. You sit down too, Daddy. This has been more of a shock to you than to anyone else, I suspect."

The elder statesmen sat side by side on the sofa, holding no communication with each other and bearing a strong resemblance to two cows in a landscape by Cuyp on the wall behind. McGrotty handed Shots a sheaf of typed paper from his folder, then went to the cocktail cabinet and mixed a gin and tonic for Ludmilla.

"Read that," Ludmilla told Shots. "It contains all the information the Report contains, but check that I'm not fooling you."

Shots glanced at the first page, the middle and one at the end, then sighed and let the sheets drift to the floor. McGrotty picked them up after handing the drink to Ludmilla.

"Secondly," said Ludmilla, "tomorrow's *Times* will announce that Mungo and I are engaged to be married. Thirdly, we four are the only people with access to the Harbinger Report. That puts us in a unique position."

"But —" said Shots, "but — but —"

The Minister said timidly, "Arthur has arranged to show Her Majesty the Report, Ludmilla."

"In half an hour!" said Shots.

"Mungo has a very good idea about that," said Ludmilla. "Tell him, Mungo."

"Arthur," said McGrotty in a voice which had no note of his former querulous bleat, "you will only upset Her Majesty if you show her the *whole* Report. Give her the dirt on the

United Kingdom but keep Europe, Asia, Africa, the Americas and Australia for ourselves."

"That notion had occurred to me," admitted Shots, "though I had intended to give her Australia and Canada."

"We cannot afford to be sentimental," said McGrotty, "Not Canada, not Australia. We deserve some recompense for our trouble, Arthur. Here is an edited version of the Report which conforms to this decision of ours. You are not named in it. You can give it to the Queen in perfect safety."

He took the manuscript Report from the briefcase and put in four typed pages of A4 size.

"I suggest, Ludmilla, that I burn this," he said, waving the original manuscript. "It is an unwieldy document and we do not need it. Our power lies not in what we can prove, but in what we know."

"Go ahead!" said Ludmilla. She loved seeing him dominate, because his power stemmed from her.

"That is not a real coal fire!" cried Shots, in pain. "It is not designed to burn things!"

"It will burn paper," said McGrotty, and it did. He stirred the ashes to powder with the poker from a stand of antique fire-irons whose function was supposed to be purely decorative.

34

"AND NOW WE MUST ALL WORK together!" said Ludmilla. "Daddy must *not* be booted into the Lords."

"Actually, Ludmilla," said the Minister, "I want to go into the Lords. Politics have become too strenuous recently. In the old days we thought nothing of a discreet phone call to our stockbrokers, but blackmail, treason and cannibalism were comparatively rare."

"Good!" said Ludmilla. "That leaves just Arthur and Mungo. Well, Arthur, make a suggestion. You have the contacts."

Shots sighed and begged, "Give me a brandy and I'll think about it."

"No, Arthur! You've had far more than enough," said McGrotty gravely.

"Don't be such a puritan, Mungo!" said Ludmilla, smiling. "Some people are improved by a little poisoning — give the old chap what he wants."

Shots sipped from the glass and said, "I suppose we can engineer a seat for McGrotty, too, at the forthcoming general election."

"Only if it's a thoroughly safe one!" said Ludmilla.

"Anyway, once he's in the House his experience will qualify him as Under Secretary for Social Stability."

"*Minister* for Social Stability," said Ludmilla.

"Don't force the pace, Ludmilla!" begged Shots. "I can put him on the front bench as soon as I'm in Number Ten, not before."

"Good!" said Ludmilla. "You can discuss the details on your way to the Palace. Mungo is going with you."

"Oh no!" wailed Shots. "How, *how* can I possibly explain your presence to —"

"Tell Her Majesty you *trust* me, Arthur. Say I'm your right-hand man," McGrotty suggested.

"Tell her that Daddy — the only completely honest Minister in her Cabinet — insisted on Mungo accompanying you, Arthur," said Ludmilla. "You don't mind us using your name, do you, Daddy?"

"Do anything you like!" cried the Minister. "But please, please tell me as little as possible."

"So you see Arthur," said Ludmilla, brightly, "there's nothing to worry about."

The phone rang. McGrotty lifted it, listened, then said, "Worry not, Miss Panther. We are ready to hit the trail."

He put the phone down, drained his glass of lemonade and said, "The car's arrived. Walky walky, Arth."

Some fibre seemed to have snapped in Arthur Shots' brain. He got to his feet like a man in his eighties rather than sixties and pointed at the briefcase with a trembling hand.

"Rereport!" he mumbled. "Rereport!"

McGrotty lifted the case in one hand, gripped Shots' forearm with the other and led him to the door. He said, "Don't worry about a thing, Arth. If you dry up I'll do the talking for us. I like Royalty. You're safe with me. So long, Bill. See you later, Ludmilla."

She blew him a kiss.

And when he had left she whirled around the room in an ecstasy of satisfaction.

"Oh, Daddy, that was glorious!" she declared. "Mungo has the makings of a really blasé political bully. He and I are going to go up and up and up. Oh, Daddy, I can't wait for the day when I sit in the Visitors' Gallery and see him rising from his seat on the front bench to refuse to answer his first question."

But her father hid his face
in his hands.

35

THE PRIME MINISTER'S RETIREMENT on the eve of a General Election was as unexpected and inadequately explained as Harold Wilson's retirement in 1977, and introduced one of those spells of flurried activity which entertain spectators without interrupting the movement of economic events. Britain had three Prime Ministers in the space of two years. The General Election returned the Tories to power with their usual safe majority and for the usual reason — Tory measures were enlarging the private wealth of leading Labour party members so they knew it was unrealistic to fight such measures, and reversing them was unthinkable. The former Chancellor of the Exchequer became Prime Minister, though political commentators suggested that the last P.M.'s colleagues had been too much her underlings for one of them to give the country an example of confident leadership. Half the press and television disagreed with this view but both halves discussed it whenever a crisis occurred. After three months the Prime Minister changed places with the Minister of Social Stability, Sir Arthur Shots.

Shots was one of the new men who had entered Parliament after the recent election, but he was not new to politics. His colleagues realised his once brilliant mind was partially damaged but this made them feel safer with him. Anyway, two previous Prime Ministers that century had been senile, two had been alcoholic and not even historians suggested this harmed the nation.* But the premiership gave Shots a new lease of life. His figure and face acquired a chubby, boyish look which reminded some people of President Kennedy and made medical observers think he was receiving a form of hormone replacement therapy. He put so much energy in pushing his Police Privatisation Bill through Parliament that, like Pitt the Elder, he collapsed of a stroke at the height of a peroration and died soon after. Maybe he had indeed been overstimulating himself with doses of a new and inadequately tested drug, for his body decomposed at a rate which struck the undertakers as supernatural. However, the coffin was lined with lead so he did not leak out during the state funeral in St Paul's.

Once more the Minister of Social Stability became Prime Minister. It was an astonishing appointment, but when astonishment died down, an obvious one. The Scottish National Party was again in an emergent phase and a Scottish Prime Minister of Britain showed the Scots that their picturesque promontary was not totally manipulated by foreigners. Also, the Tory party depends as much as any other on voters who labour with their hands. It was good to show the employed part of the British workforce that the

---

* *Ramsay MacDonald and Winston Churchill were senile in their later years: Herbert Asquith and Churchill were alcoholic.*

son of a charlady could, with honest toil and a spark of talent, be advised by the Queen on the running of the country. It also showed the world that Britain was not ruled by an old, unfair and corrupt system of social classification based on inherited wealth. And Mungo McGrotty was the kind of Scot folk instinctively trusted. On television he looked and sounded guileless, almost vulnerable, but also hopeful, firm and wise. He had not much humour and made little jokes about this, but he had a very beautiful young wife. Old ladies wept happy tears over newspaper pictures of McGrotty and Ludmilla: they were so obviously proud of each other, and no such loving couple had been prominent in British politics since the days of Edward VIII and Mrs Simpson. McGrotty also had a personal but effective parliamentary style which was well shown in his handling of the debate on the Harbinger Report.

36

A YEAR EARLIER, *PRIVATE EYE* HAD hinted at the strange disappearance of a Report to which several public servants had contributed, a Report which had led to nothing but the unexplained suicide of an innocent and well-liked man. As the event moved further into the past other papers referred to this and the *New Statesman* published an article headed "What Became of Harbinger?" Questions were asked in Parliament, though nobody on the front bench admitted or denied that a Report had existed.

"On this topic we have been fed nothing but a diet of rumours, excuses and prevarications!" cried a Labour MP who was sometimes suspected of socialism. "What has become of the Harbinger Report? When will the people of Britain be told the truth by their elected representatives?"

"Like most of the Labour Party, The Right Honourable Member for Tonypandy is clearly living in the past," said the Prime Minister. "The Harbinger Report was specifically conceived as a secret weapon to deal with some defects in our organisation without inconveniencing parliament or wasting public time. That secret weapon was one hundred per cent effective. It repaired these defects. In secret."

("Oh! Oh! Oh! Oh!" howled and groaned the Opposition benches. Someone screamed, "Liar!")

McGrotty smiled thinly and raised his voice. "A few Civil Servants who put private gain before public welfare were quietly and very effectively disciplined. There the matter would have ended had not the author of the Report, Geoffrey Harbinger, come to feel as guilty as those he condemned. If you cannot imagine a public servant of excellent credentials being infected by suspicion when heading a controversial investigation, I will remind you of the Stalker Inquiry."

("That was a ramp as well!" bellowed the Shadow Home Secretary, and a back-bench Tory bellowed, "It was your ramp as much as ours!")

"I accuse Geoffrey Harbinger of nothing!" cried the Prime Minister. "I respect him! Any wrong he did was wiped out by his decision to pay the supreme penalty. It would be disgusting and vindictive to say more just now about Harbinger and his Report. The dead man's innocent relations are still among us — I am speaking about a widow-woman and a wee girl. GEOFFREY'S SISTER AND NIECE STILL LOVE HIM EVEN IF YOU DON'T!" he suddenly roared, and stood erect, glaring at the ceiling, fists clenched at sides, every line in his body showing indignation at the persecution of innocents. Instant silence fell. The debate was being televised. Many members were cowed by the point he had made, others were totally staggered by McGrotty. Surely there must be more to him than intelligent hypocrisy? But what more could there be?

He used the silence to wind up the debate very quietly. "I suggest this House has more urgent matters to discuss. Inflation. The greed of the Unions. Drug abuse. The Aids

epidemic. Local Government dictatorship, lesbian
conspiracies against the Defence of our Realm and
international terrorist conspiracies to destroy law, order,
peace, freedom and common human decency both abroad
and here! Here in Britain. The decent people of Britain have
chosen us to help and protect them. They deserve that from
us, at the very least. That's our job. Let's do it. It's a lot more
important than this storm in a Civil Service teacup."

He had never sounded more like an ordinary, down-to-
earth, sensible Scotsman, yet the camera lens zoomed in on
a *spiritual* face: gaunt, bearded, calm, strong, and somehow
tragic. "Christlike!" was the word which sprang unbidden to
a million viewers' minds. Ludmilla, gazing raptly at the
screen in a room of their Hampstead residence (her father
had left it to enter a sanitorium), made a small, ardent
moaning sound.

She could hardly wait for McGrotty
to return to her.

ACKNOWLEDGEMENTS

ONCE UPON A TIME A PRODUCER of television plays planned a series of them based upon popular nursery tales, but in modern settings. *Goldilocks and the Three Bears,* for instance, became the story of an innocent young social worker who visited an unemployed family and hardly escaped with her life. Told of this project by my London literary agent, Francis Head, I imagined the Aladdin story with the hero a junior civil servant, wicked uncle Abanazir a senior one, and the magic lamp a secret government paper which gave whoever held it unlimited powers of blackmail. The television producer rejected the idea so I made of it a radio play which Francis sold to London BBC. Directed by Shaun McLaughlin, *McGrotty and Ludmilla, or The Harbinger Report* was broadcast on the 18th of July, 1975. I give the date to show that, though a blatant plagiarist, I did not plagiarise the Whitehall comedy programme *Yes, Minister.*

The plot of my romance is from *Arabian Nights,* but I first discovered the world it shows in *But Soft — We Are Observed,* a satire on the British state written by Hilaire

Belloc, illustrated by G.K. Chesterton, and first published in 1928. Like most political satire, from Aristophanes' *Wasps* to Pohl and Kombluth's *The Space Merchants,* it is set ahead of the author's time. Belloc describes Britain under the premiership of Mary Bull, leader of the Anarchist party. The Anarchists speak out for the freedom of the individual, and are the successors of the Unionists who were previously Conservatives and originally Tories. The official opposition (which speaks for social justice and equality) are the Communists, formerly the Labour party, who succeded the Liberals who began as Whigs. The leaders of both parties unite to maintain the unearned incomes of the British investing classes, for they belong to them. The government and opposition connive to get profitable contracts for wealthy corporations while pretending in parliament to protect equal freedom and justice for everyone under the rule of law. This means big government transactions are made under a cloak of secrecy, a cloak held in place by magistrates, the police and various spy networks. These networks, like all unions of cheats and liars, are incompetent and treacherous, but hurt their victims more than their employers.

The hero of the book is a guileless young man and new to London. The secret intelligence agencies (one of them American) mistake him for the emissary of an eastern oil-bearing country, a place whose bandit chiefs will be recognised as a government by other governments as soon as they sell their mineral rights to western corporations. The perplexed hero is swiftly brought to palatial offices and homes where he meets the chief manipulators of British finance, news and politics. Unlike Mungo McGrotty he never understands his false position well enough to exploit it. His ignorance is mistaken for cunning. To stop him dealing with other people he is sent to jail for resisting police harassment, and only released when the real emissary arrives in Britain: a devious Asiatic broker who talks in terms the British chiefs understand perfectly.

When I read this novel in the fifties I thought it a funny but out-of-date caricature of an obsolete system. In the late forties the British Labour party, without violent revolution or dictatorship, had established (I believed) a working alternative to monopoly capitalism. Most education and health care, all broadcasting, most transport, fuel, power and a lot of housing were funded and owned by our local and national governments, who were supposed to put the good of all before the profit of some. The British Common wealth (wealth held in common) was larger than it had been since the privatisation of the common lands in the eighteenth and early nineteenth century. The nineteen fifties was a time of full employment, when many of the rich whined publicly about how poor they were. Evelyn Waugh, comparing life in those days with his golden memories of pre-war Britain, said he felt he was living "in an occupied country" — a catchphrase which then meant *a country conquered by outsiders.* I thought great riches and poverty had been abolished in Britain: that no important politicians had secrets worth hiding: that most secret agents were inventions of fiction writers. I thought Britain an unusually decent country. I did not know that this Britain was in a temporary state of reaction to the huge indecency of the Second World War and the indecency of the Depression which led to it.

Since then national and local British governments have connived to sell the Common wealth to private speculators for the profits they will make. Our national health and education services have become shabby beggars pleading for alms. Our district councils are no longer funded by a Victorian rates system which taxed richer properties more highly: we have a Hanoverian poll tax to which rich and poor pay the same. At each phase of the Common wealth sell-off Labour leaders have silenced, or rejected as extremist, those supporters who want public reacquisition put on the party's programme in terms which would discourage shareholders. The leaders explain that it can only come to power with the help of people the Tory policies have made richer, so the more right-wing the Tory party has become, the more right-wing the Labour party has become. On every major issue which divided the two main British parties (nuclear disarmament, entry into Europe, self-rule for Scotland) the Labour and Tory leaders have been on the same side. The only political fun has been the public scandals over our spy system. Since the scandal of Burgess and Maclean, each subsequent revelation has shown that our spy systems are larger, richer, more active and incompetent than we thought possible, and more essential to our government's operations. They are *not,* however, essential because the government has important secrets to hide from foreign enemies. They are declared essential because they prevent most British people learning and discussing decisions made, things done for the defence and benefit (we are told) of themselves.

Orwell made horrid fun of life under any modern dictatorship by caricaturing Britain during the wartime coalition. In *But Soft — We Are Observed* Belloc caricatured Britain as it usually is: a plutocracy pretending to be a democracy by manipulating a two-party assembly which offers voters little to choose between but styles of rhetoric. Indeed, it now looks more like a sober portrait than a caricature. My novella is certainly a caricature, though it caricatures nothing but the ability of the British rich to enlist awkward or threatening outsiders.

In February 1987, the stage version of *McGrotty and Ludmilla* was produced by Michael Boyd at the Tron Theatre, Glasgow, with this cast:

Mungo McGrotty	Kevin McMonigle
Arthur Shots	Russell Hunter
Ludmilla	Julia St John
Ms Panther, Bee, Mary Fox	Vivienne Dixon
The Minister	Sandy Neilson
Aubrey Rose, American artist	Bill Murdoch
Charlie Gold, Harbinger	Sean Scanlon

Peter Ling designed the set and the production suggested details for this book. Arthur Shots' global cocktail cabinet, McGrotty's bottle of booze brought to the wrong kind of party, Ludmilla's riding habit and sexual employment of drugs were devised by one of those named above, or by some of them in conjunction. And McGrotty's face on the front jacket is copied from Kevin McMonigle in the part.

In Chapter 32 the distortion of Lord Acton's axiom on power is taken from Pohl and Kornbluth's fine novel *The Space Merchants*.

To furnish Chapter 33 I stole a Dutch landscape with cows from *Little Dorrit*. My heavy villain's lapse into blank verse (in Chapter 32) when deeply excited is from Thackeray's *The Rose and The Ring*. So (I suspect) is my assumption that

most very powerful people, like all the rest of us, are moved
by the appetites of greedy adolescents, but do more damage
with them.

I will look kindly upon the advances of producers who
think *McGrotty and Ludmilla* would make a good television
film, but the advances should be made through my present
London agent, Xandra Hardie. Francis Head died of lung
cancer in 1978. She smoked a lot. I wish she had not died,
but cannot wish she had smoked less. I found her helpful,
tolerant, and enjoyable company.

Deliberate abstinence might have
soured some of that.

GOODBYE

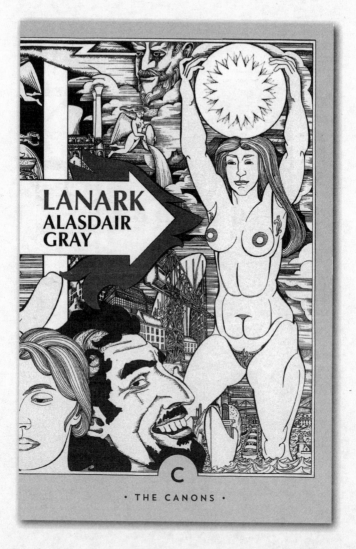

LANARK
ALASDAIR
GRAY

'Probably the greatest novel of the century'
Observer

CANON‖GATE

THE FALL OF KELVIN WALKER

BY ALASDAIR GRAY

• THE CANONS •

'Bawdy and exuberant'
Guardian

CANON GATE

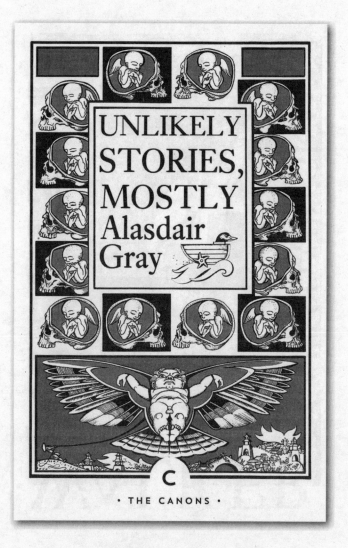

UNLIKELY STORIES, MOSTLY

Alasdair Gray

• THE CANONS •

'Unsettling, otherworldly'
Financial Times

CANON█GATE